HARD HIT

A ST. LOUIS MAVERICKS HOCKEY ROMANCE

BRENDA ROTHERT

KAT MIZERA

CHAPTER ONE

Boone

I opened my eyes, blinking to bring the face just inches from mine into focus. When I saw the enthusiasm in her expression, I suppressed a groan.

"Good morning, handsome," she said softly. "What are we going to do today?"

Damn, I'd done it again. I'd fallen asleep after a couple of hours of sex with a woman I'd just met instead of leaving. I knew better. And now I had to deal with the fallout.

"Oh, hey," I said, sitting up. "I didn't mean to fall asleep. Sorry about that."

Cami smiled sweetly. Or was it Katie? Shit. It was definitely Katie.

"Oh, no worries. I'm off work today so whatever you feel like doing…I'm game."

She snuggled up to my bare back and a wave of guilt hit me. I'd assumed that when she asked if I wanted to get to know her better at the bar we'd met at, while unbuttoning her shirt, that she was thinking casual sex, like me.

It was always more with women, though. Even when they said no strings, there were *always* strings.

"I'm actually busy today," I said, patting her hand to signal she should move it so I could get up. "I have to go to a wedding. But last night was great. Thanks."

Katie didn't miss a beat.

"Oh, I love weddings! And I have the perfect dress!"

I'd done this to myself by falling asleep. I just hoped I could undo it without having anything hurled at my head on the way out the door.

"It's a…" I cleared my throat, picking up my jeans from the floor and stepping into them. "It's my coach's daughter, actually. And the team…we're like family. I can't just invite someone."

Katie slid out of bed and walked over to her closet.

"I'm *great* at weddings," she gushed from inside the small walk-in closet. "I was a bridesmaid three times last year. I'm basically a pro."

She wasn't making this easy. I quickly threw on my T-shirt and laced up my shoes so I could haul ass out the door. I grabbed my wallet and keys just as Katie came out of the closet with a dress in each hand.

"Pink or red?" she asked.

"I have to run," I said. "Got to grab some coffee. But last night was great, so—"

"Oh, I can make coffee." She discarded the dresses on her bed. "And I can make waffles, too. You do like waffles, right?"

I glanced at my watch. Shit, it was later than I thought.

"Listen, I really have to go," I said.

"But—"

"I only RSVP'd for one to the wedding, and I'm not looking for a relationship, so…"

Her hopeful expression slid away. "Oh. You should have been open about that, Boone."

"I wasn't *not* open about it. You came over to me and my friends and we had some drinks, and then you asked if I wanted to get to know you better. You brought me home and we had a good time."

She sighed softly. "I'd be a really good girlfriend for a professional athlete, though. I've been thinking about it since I woke up, picturing me at your games and at charity events."

I nodded, mentally kicking myself for drinking so much beer I'd been too tired to get up and leave after the sex.

"If I wanted a girlfriend, I'm sure you would be a good one," I said, walking out of her bedroom. "Thanks again, Katie. I really did have fun."

"It's Cami!"

Shit. Now she was pissed. I picked up the pace, making it to the front door and getting my hand on the handle before I felt the thunk of something hitting my back. A black shoe with a high heel landed on the ground next to me.

"Asshole!" Cami cried. "Get out of here."

"I'm trying, but"

The fucking dead bolt wouldn't open. I pushed and pushed, but nothing. Briefly, a *Misery*-situation with a woman who wanted me to marry her to avoid being maimed flashed through my mind. I had to stop falling asleep like this.

"It sticks," Cami said with a huff, pushing me out of the way.

She pushed on the door with her shoulder and slid the dead bolt open. I opened the door and darted out without another word, keeping my head down.

"I don't even like hockey!" Cami yelled at my back. "Real men play football!"

That was a low blow, but I still didn't engage. I had to get my ass home and get ready for Coach's daughter's wedding. I couldn't risk inviting his ire by being late.

———

An hour later, I was shaved, showered, and dressed in a charcoal suit paired with a light blue dress shirt and a navy tie, turning into the parking lot of the church in Ladue, a St. Louis suburb where the wedding was being held.

Hopefully this wedding would be short and sweet and we wouldn't get stuck waiting hours for the wedding party to take photos before we could eat. I was ravenous—borderline hangry.

With so many teammates getting married the past couple of years, I had the wedding routine down. Show up, smile, eat, dance, possibly hook up with a bridesmaid. And don't cheap out on the gift.

Jolie Gizzard's parents had plenty of money—Coach Gizzard was very well paid—so I'd gone with a gift of $500, which was what most of the other guys on the team were giving. I had a stack of wedding cards in a drawer at home so I never had to run around at the last minute picking one up. Totally my assistant's idea. I never thought about that stuff.

The parking lot was packed and I didn't see anyone walking from their car into the church.

Shit. I was late. I had to find a spot quickly and get inside.

I was circling the lot a second time when the sight of a woman running toward me made me slow down. Was that…?

Oh hell. *Fucking* hell. It was Jolie Gizzard, the bride. I'd only met her a couple of times at team events when she was with Coach, but I recognized her bright red hair immediately. Also, she was likely the only woman here wearing a wedding dress.

Why was she running toward my car, though? I slowed to a stop and looked in my rearview mirror to see if maybe she was running toward something behind me. There was nothing, though.

I rolled down my passenger window and leaned over as she arrived at my car, breathless. She tried the door handle and found it locked, her eyes widening in panic.

"Open it, Boone!" she said.

"What's going on?"

"There's no time! Open the fucking door!"

She was frantic, the tears streaming down her face tinged with black eye makeup. Christ, this could only be one thing—a runaway bride situation. And I was sure as hell not going to be seen driving away from this church with Gizzard's daughter in my car. I needed a trade to Nashville, so staying on my coach's good side was imperative.

"Calm down," I said, putting a palm up.

Jolie narrowed her eyes at me. "*You* calm down, asshole. I said open this door. Open it right now!"

She kept pulling on the handle of my Range Rover, which was making me feel as panicked as she looked. My car was my most prized possession. After saving nearly every cent I made my first four years in the NHL in case I got injured and couldn't play anymore, I'd splurged on this car.

"Hey, let up on the handle," I said.

"Then open it!"

Jolie was usually mild-mannered, smiling and making small talk about hockey. I'd never seen her like this.

"Boone, I *have* to get out of here," she pleaded.

"Well, I have to keep my balls attached to my body, so I can't be seen leaving here with you when you're supposed to be getting married" I looked down at my watch. "Right now."

She exhaled through her nose, lasering me with a death glare. "I don't want to go through with this wedding. If you have any semblance of a soul, you will open this door and help me."

Shit. Everyone knew Coach loved his future son-in-law. I'd be at the top of his shit list if I whisked his daughter away from this wedding.

I had a sister, though, and if she were in this situation...I'd want someone to help her.

Shaking my head, I pushed the button to unlock the door. Jolie immediately opened it and got in, pulling yards of pale pink fabric into the car before closing the door.

"Get down," I hissed. "I don't want anyone to see you."

She knitted her brows together. "Well, either that'll work, or someone will see us and think I'm giving you a blow job."

"Fuck!" I slammed my hand against the steering wheel. "Don't get down!"

I threw the vehicle into reverse and looked in the rearview mirror as I backed up, eager to get out of here as quickly as possible.

"You're getting me into the deepest pile of shit ever," I grumbled as I turned the wheel near the parking lot entrance.

"Well, you're getting me *out* of the deepest pile of shit ever," she lobbed back. "And it's your own fault for running late."

I glared at her. "Maybe it's your fault for deciding not to get married a minute and a half before the wedding was supposed to start."

"It's done now, and I don't care what you or anyone else think."

Her shaky voice deflated my anger in an instant. She was right—she was going to face a shitload of anger and criticism over this decision, and she didn't need more from me, someone she didn't even know.

"Where am I taking you?" I asked.

She blew out a breath. "My apartment is in the Loop."

"Okay." I shifted in my seat and looked over at her. "You okay?"

Her laugh was weary. "Not really. But I will be. I know this was the right decision."

"Do you need to call someone? Just to let them know that you're okay? They'll be looking for you."

"I left a note."

I nodded and we drove in silence for a couple of minutes. Suddenly, she turned to me, her face still streaked black but dry now.

"He said I'm a practical choice," she said. "Last night at our rehearsal dinner, I overheard him talking to one of his friends when he didn't know I was nearby. He said now that he's in his thirties, he decided to choose someone solid instead of sexy."

Jesus, what kind of man said that about the woman he was marrying? Jolie was a tall, lithe redhead with a killer smile. She was damn sexy, and

I was one of several guys on my team who would have made a play for her if she hadn't been our coach's daughter.

"I'm sorry," I said, unable to come up with anything else.

She exhaled heavily and leaned back into the seat. "I feel like shit about all of this. I should have called it off sooner. Last night wasn't the first time I had reservations. And my parents spent a ton on the wedding." She laughed, but it sounded more weary than amused. "Maybe you should take me to a bar instead of home. Checking out of my head for a few hours would be great."

"Is that what you want?"

"No." Her tone was defeated. "I want to go home and take off this dress and never see it again."

"Okay."

She looked over at me and smiled. "Thanks for this. I'll tell my dad I jumped into your car and left you no choice."

I shrugged. "He's still going to murder me."

"I won't let him."

She didn't know that Coach had the power to keep me from what I wanted most in the world, and that now, he probably would. I drove in silence, knowing I had to make the best of things while still playing in St. Louis.

CHAPTER TWO

Jolie

I HADN'T BEEN HOME in several days since I'd been staying at my parents' house through all the last-minute wedding plans and events. Jarvis had been staying there too, until last night, since the bride and groom weren't supposed to see each other before the wedding. He'd been more than happy to go to the downtown hotel where his friends and teammates who were coming to the wedding were staying. In retrospect, he'd been far more excited to hang out with my dad than with me the last few weeks, and I wasn't sure when I'd stopped ignoring all the red flags.

His complete disinterest in my studies.

The way he vacationed with his friends during the off-season, always coming up with a reason why I'd be happier home or in my lab.

His lack of excitement in the wedding planning.

Our lackluster sex life.

I carefully laid my dress on the bed, staring at it sadly.

The one thing I'd been excited about had been this damn dress.

A pink champagne color instead of true white because it looked so much better against my incredibly pale skin, and it fit me perfectly without any alterations. The tight bodice accentuated my small waist and pushed up my breasts, giving the illusion of cleavage. The full, Cinderella-style skirt hid my round hips and made me look tall, busty, and elegant, something I'd always wanted to be.

Too bad Jarvis wouldn't get to appreciate what he was missing out on.

After I'd undressed, I stepped under the hot shower spray and closed my eyes, letting the water wash away the pain and humiliation of the day. I probably only had a few minutes before someone found me, but I was over it at this point.

Jarvis had never been my choice and I couldn't understand why I'd allowed myself to be pushed into dating a man that clearly wasn't into me. Hell, I wasn't really all that into him.

My father had wanted this match and I'd figured it was a good time to get married.

I'd also been a little starry-eyed in the beginning.

Handsome, rich, hotshot hockey players didn't usually look twice at a tall redhead who was far more interested in microbiology and the specimens in my lab than men.

Not that I didn't like men. I did. I just didn't have a lot of patience for them. And the athletes I'd been around my entire life because of my father had reminded me of Neanderthals. I was probably being a little bitchy by lumping all men together like that, but single young hockey players could be the worst kind of womanizers. I'd seen it firsthand, heard my dad talking about it, and joked about it with my friends.

I wasn't sure why I'd assumed it would be different with Jarvis.

Because my father had picked him?

Ew.

The more I thought about it, the more annoyed I got.

I'd just pulled on my bathrobe when someone banged on the front door loudly and insistently.

Jarvis.

Oh goody.

I was so looking forward to having it out with him.

Not.

I hadn't washed my hair since I'd just washed it this morning and the salon had done a gorgeous job blowing it out, so I left it in its elegant updo as I padded to the door.

"For god's sake, Jarvis, you don't have to alert the media that you're here."

"What the fuck, Jolie?" He exploded into the room, the tails of his tuxedo swinging as he paced. "Are you kidding me with this last-minute jitter bullshit?"

"It's really not that last minute, and we're way beyond jitters."

He turned, glaring at me. "Why? I've fucking given you everything. I let you plan the wedding of your dreams and—"

"You *let* me?" I countered, folding my arms. "You mean you were relieved you didn't have to participate in a single detail so you could party with your friends until the very last minute?"

He narrowed his eyes. "What did I do to upset you now? You're always pissed off about something. It's exhausting trying to never do anything that hurts your feelings. Is there anything that makes you happy other than your precious lab rats?"

I gritted my teeth. He knew damn well I didn't use rats in my lab, but he liked to say that. Incessantly.

"Well, whatever it is, it's not you," I said finally. "You don't make me happy, and obviously I don't make you happy. You should be glad I've saved us both the time, expense, and headache of a divorce a year or two from now."

"Goddamn it." He threw up his hands. "I told your father this would never work, but he said you'd settle down once we were married because you wanted babies. What changed, Jolie? Yesterday we were happy."

I sighed. I loved my father, but he'd never really gotten over the fact that his only child was a girl. When it had become clear I was never going to be a professional athlete, I guessed he'd assumed my marrying one would be the next best thing. I had no intention of marrying anyone anytime soon, and even if I did somehow end up with an athlete, it wasn't going to be this one.

"Look." I opted to throw myself under the bus just to get this over with. "This is all my fault and I'll deal with the fallout. I'll send back the gifts, write notes to everyone and apologize. Whatever has to be done, I'll take the blame for everything. You can go back to Chicago and let the world know I broke your heart. I'm sure it won't take you long to replace me."

"Jolie. Babe. Come on. You know that's not what I want."

Obviously, he was trying another tactic, using his softer, sweeter side, the one that had gotten me to go out with him in the first place. I knew better now, though. Soft, sweet Jarvis only showed up when he wanted something.

"Jarvis, stop, okay? Just stop. I know you don't love me and I'm not in love with you either. I made this decision for both of us, no matter what you might think."

"What are you talking about?" He stared at me angrily, his dark eyes suddenly filled with confusion. "How can you say I don't—"

"I heard you talking to Manny last night. I know *exactly* how you feel about me." I met his gaze without blinking, waiting for it to sink in.

We were done.

Completely and totally done.

———

I WAS USED to letting my father down. I'd long since stopped worrying about that. Disappointing my mother was something else entirely. She'd been crying all morning and I hated being the cause. There was no help for this, though. Hopefully, she'd get over it after another day or two.

After Jarvis and I had talked, my parents had come over. Once I'd explained everything, Dad got pissed off all over again and went looking for Jarvis. Mom had stayed with me at the apartment, trying to find a way to change my mind and coming up with dozens of excuses for Jarvis. It was almost comical how much people who didn't really know him liked him. Ironically, the one person who'd taken my side was my paternal grandmother.

Grandma G, which was what I'd always called her, was eighty-one and still spry and active. She'd never liked Jarvis and based on the story I'd heard from one of my bridesmaids, she'd hooted with laughter when the announcement had been made that the wedding was off.

Today she was in my parents' sunroom having brunch with me, my mother, and my Aunt Nita, who was my mother's sister. Grandma G lived in an assisted living facility not far from here, but Aunt Nita lived in Boston, so she'd come to town for the wedding and I liked spending time with her.

"Sometimes things happen for a reason," Aunt Nita said after my mother started sniffling again. "You can't know it now, but there's probably someone amazing out there for you, Jolie. Mark my words."

I grimaced. "I am zero percent interested in dating. I want to get my PhD before I even think about any of that again."

"You and Jarvis can work things out," Mom said. "He's sorry. He didn't mean what he said to Manny. You know how guys are. They try to act all aloof in front of their friends, like they don't have emotions, but that's just—"

"Horrible," I said, interrupting her. "And I don't want to spend my life with a man who thinks it's *cool* to tell his friends he doesn't find his fiancée sexy. Besides, I'm not in love with him, and I don't want that for him. He shouldn't settle any more than I should." Okay, that might've been a tiny lie, since I didn't give a shit about Jarvis anymore, but it might get my mother to settle down.

"Couldn't you learn to love him?" she asked.

"Tammy!" Aunt Nita looked shocked. "This isn't the 1950s. She shouldn't have to force herself to love someone. There are lots of fish in the sea."

"Besides, he sucks in the sack," Grandma G said.

"If I'd known that before now, I wouldn't have *let* her marry him."

I bit my lip to keep from laughing as Mom gasped and Aunt Nita dipped her head.

"Mom!" My mother glared at her mother-in-law.

"Okay, we're not going to talk about my sex life," I said, quickly changing the subject. I'd blurted out that little tidbit about our sex life this morning when I'd first gotten here; leave it to Grandma G not to miss a thing. "I'm really sorry I waited until the eleventh hour to cancel the wedding, but it wasn't until I heard him talking to his friend that I realized all those red flags had been my subconscious warning me. He doesn't love me, not really, and I don't love him either. It would have been a disaster. I did us all a favor."

"Your father is very upset," Mom said, lifting her coffee cup and meeting my gaze over the rim. "You're going to have to talk to him."

"I know."

"It would go a long way to making him happy if you volunteered for the kids' camp coming up," she said.

"I've got a lot to do at the lab," I protested. He'd asked me every year if I would help him coach at the hockey camp for underprivileged kids that he spon-sored, and I'd always made excuses.

Mom gave me a look. "Your non-wedding cost us tens of thousands of dollars. I think the least you could do is help your father with the camp. He and different guys from the team deal with the older kids, but he needs help with the younger ones, especially the girls. You know how gruff he is and the little ones are scared of him."

I thought about it for a minute and realized it might not just help mend fences with my dad but also get me out of the lab once in a while. I spent far too much time there, and though I loved what I was working on, my body was starting to protest all the time I spent hunched over a microscope or in front of my computer. Exercise combined with keeping Dad off my back was a win-win deal.

Not to mention, I loved hockey.

I'd played when I was younger, until my love for science had overshadowed everything else. It might be fun to get back out on the ice. And I loved kids, so that part wouldn't be a problem.

First thing tomorrow, I'd talk to my dad.

Maybe then things could go back to some semblance of normal.

CHAPTER THREE

Boone

I'D NEVER BEEN a person who prayed, but as the phone rang, I closed my eyes and asked God to heal Andy. To give him the strength he needed to get through the fight of his life.

"Hey, man," my brother said when he answered my call.

"Hey. You answered. That's a good sign."

His laugh was gruff, without a note of amusement. "I'm too fucking sick to even sleep. This round kicked my ass."

Why? I'd asked the universe that question hundreds of times in the past three months. Why did my younger brother have to battle colon cancer when he'd just married the love of his life two years ago? When he'd become a father one year ago? It was so damn unfair.

"Worse than the time we swiped Dad's huge bottle of whiskey and drank the whole thing?" I asked.

Andy groaned. "Shit, man, I thought I was going to die that day."

I'd puked into a football helmet from my bed, too sick to even make it to the bathroom. I'd been seventeen and Andy had been fifteen. It had taken me years to be able to even look at whiskey without feeling ill.

"Dad was so fucking pissed." I smiled at the memory. "You told him the hangover was punishment enough."

"Yeah, he didn't agree."

It was brutal being so far away from my brother when he was going through hell. I could hear the exhaustion in his tone. My agent was looking into the possibility of a trade to Nashville, my hometown, so I could be closer to Andy, but each day that passed felt like forever.

"How's Carrie doing?" I asked.

Andy sighed into the phone. "She's doing it all. I can't do shit. She's up at night with Mason, then up early to feed him breakfast and get him to day care.

When she gets home from work, she has to take care of me and him and the house."

For my brother, the hardest part of having cancer was being helpless. He'd been a broad-shouldered construction worker. A CrossFitter. An avid hunter. An active father. And now he weighed a buck sixty, his body suffering the effects of both cancer and his treatment.

When I got back to Nashville, I'd be able to help take some of the load off of Carrie. I wanted to be there for her and my nephew as much as I wanted to be there for my brother.

"For the eightieth time, she needs to quit her job," I said, rubbing my forehead in irritation. "I have the money for everything you guys need."

Andy exhaled heavily. "We need the health insurance, though. And I can't take that kind of money from you."

A flare of helpless anger rose in my chest. "You're my brother. I don't give a shit about the money. What's the point of the money if I can't help my family with it?"

"This treatment will end up costing hundreds of thousands, man."

"I've got it," I fired back. "I've got plenty of money in the bank. If I can't physically be there to help right now, this is the only thing in my power that I can do. Let me."

"Fuck," he muttered. "I'm gonna be sick. Look, I'll talk to her, but we're okay on money and I think working gets her mind off of me, which is good. We're good."

I wanted to beat my phone against the kitchen counter. We'd been having this conversation since his diagnosis, and I'd only made a shred of headway.

"She can go part time, then," I said. "I'm at the point where you guys can either take money from me, or I'm quitting hockey to move in with you. I'll be around all the time. All the time."

"Michael," Andy said, his voice strong and stern now. "That is not a fucking option. Promise me you won't do that. I'd never forgive myself."

I looked up at the ceiling, at my wits' end. "Put yourself in my shoes."

"I have to go," he said. "We'll talk later."

His voice was tinged with agony as he ended the call. All I wanted was to quit hockey and go be with him. So far, the treatment seemed to be helping, but Andy could be in the final months of his life, and I hated that I had to be so far from him.

Dad had passed away four years ago and Mom did everything she could to help Andy and Carrie. Our sister Emma had taken off with her shitty boyfriend five years ago and we hadn't heard from her since, other than our parents getting an occasional call asking for money. I needed to be home, and soon.

For now, I had to shake off my bad mood because it was Tuesday, and that meant I had an evening youth hockey practice.

Time to put on my game face. I'd developed a pretty great one over the past couple of months.

I DID a double take when I skated onto the ice at the youth hockey rink and saw Jolie Gizzard talking to a group of girls. What was she doing here?

Coach Gizzard was just a few feet away from her, so I assumed he had something to do with it.

Fucking great. The last thing I needed was for her to say something to me, or even look at me, and make Gizzard suspicious.

"Boone, watch!" a little boy named Lucas called out.

He was a little guy—five years old—but he had boundless energy and every time he fell, he got up and tried even harder.

Lucas skated his fastest to the wall, then turned around and skated back to me.

"Nice," I said, offering him a high five.

"Did you see how fast I went?" he asked.

I gave him a mock skeptical look. "You're trying to steal my job, aren't you?"

He laughed and nodded.

"Okay, gather up," Coach Gizzard called.

I stayed off to the side, sneaking a glance at Jolie as Coach talked to the kids. She was comfortable on skates, which wasn't surprising for a hockey coach's daughter. Wearing leggings with an oversized hoodie, a sweater headband covering her ears and matching blue gloves on her hands, she looked even better to me than she had on her wedding day.

Not only was she a smoking-hot redhead, but she also wasn't one of those high-maintenance women who wouldn't be caught dead on an ice rink in comfortable clothes. The fingers of her gloves were cut off, so I could see she didn't have fake nails. No fake lashes, either.

One of the little girls she'd been talking to skated over to Jolie and hugged her around the waist. She smiled down at her, put an arm around her, and went back to listening to her dad.

I forced myself to look at my teammate Nash, who also volunteered coaching here. The last thing I needed was to get caught staring at Coach's daughter.

She was on the rebound, making her ripe for a fling. But she was my coach's daughter.

Coach dismissed everyone to start drills, and I groaned inwardly when Jolie and I were assigned to the same group, standing side by side and feeding pucks.

"Hey," she said.

"Hey, how's it going?"

"Pretty good. Thanks again for…you know."

I nodded. "No problem."

I dumped out our bucket of pucks to make our work easier. She fed a puck to the first skater, then I slid the next one toward her.

"It's been a hot second since I had a stick in my hand," she said lightly.

She knew what she was doing, no matter how long it had been.

"You play hockey?" I asked.

"Oh yeah. My dad wanted me to be the first female in the big league."

"Hang on, guys," Nash said to us. "I want to show them something real quick."

I turned to Jolie as Nash demonstrated stickhandling form to the kids in our group. "I take it you didn't want that?"

She laughed. "No. I was done with hockey by my

sophomore year of high school, but my dad made me play through the end of senior year."

"Hey, did you tell him about…?"

"Yeah, I told him I jumped in your car and pretty much forced you to give me a ride. Don't worry, it's me he's mad at, not you."

"Still?"

It had been several days since the wedding that wasn't. I wondered how long Coach would stay pissed. He was known for holding grudges, but Jolie was his only daughter.

She shrugged. "I think he thinks Jarvis and I are going to patch things up and elope."

I suppressed a groan. She'd dodged a bullet already. Why would she jump out in front of another one?

"Are you?" I asked.

She shook her head. "Absolutely not. I'm done."

"But your dad wants to change your mind," I said.

She gave me a knowing smile. "He can be stubborn, but you probably know that."

I laughed because that was an understatement. Coach Gizzard had once made me skate the same drill for two hours when he was pissed off about how I'd played in a game the night before. When he had his mind made up about something, there was no changing it.

"Is this part of your probation?" I asked her.

"Pretty much. My mom called it a peace offering. But I don't mind, honestly. It feels good to be out on the ice again."

Nash resumed the drill, and Jolie and I returned to feeding pucks.

"Jarvis giving you any trouble?" I asked her.

"Nothing I can't handle."

"He'll find a puck bunny to distract himself."

After a single note of laughter, Jolie said, "I'm sure he already has. He's back in Chicago and I don't plan to see him ever again."

"Hope it blows over with your dad."

"Thanks. If he wants to stay pissed about it, it's okay. I'll just avoid him. He'll get over it eventually."

We were split up for the next drill, Jolie working with her dad and his group of kids while Nash and I gently shot pucks at kids as they stood in goal. The excitement of the kids over the smallest things cracked me up and got my mind off of what my brother was going through.

"Boys, come on over," Gizzard said to me and Nash after practice had ended and we were the only ones left on the rink.

"Coach, we can round these up," I said, meaning the pucks all three of us were gathering.

"Yeah, do that and get everything put away in the equipment room, would you?" he said.

"No problem."

Hell, I'd shine his shoes to stay on his good side. As soon as my agent got back to me about the prospects for a trade, I planned to have a one-on-one conversation with Coach and tell him what was going on with my brother. If he knew why I wanted the trade, he'd be more likely to work with me.

"My daughter is here helping, but don't get any ideas," Coach said. "She's taken."

"Jolie?" I said, confused about what he meant.

He narrowed his eyes at me. "That better be the last time I hear her name come out of your mouth, Boone. Don't talk to her, don't talk about her, don't even look at her."

Nash scoffed. "Coach, I'm not even single."

"I'm just letting you both know so we're clear." His gaze never left me. "She's going through a hard time right now and she's vulnerable. But she has a fiancé. If I find out you're sniffing around, you'll wish you wouldn't have."

"Wouldn't dream of it, Coach," I said smoothly.

"Yeah, same," Nash said, sounding offended. "Like I said, I have a girlfriend."

Coach Gizzard didn't even acknowledge us

further. He could be a dick, and clearly his daughter was a sore spot for him.

"I thought Jolie dumped Jarvis," Nash said to me under his breath as we gathered pucks.

"Yeah, she did."

He laughed. "Giz didn't get the memo?"

"Oh, he got it. I think he decided to shred it and completely disregard the fact that Jolie was unhappy."

"Shit. Poor Jolie."

"Yeah."

She was going to have her hands full dealing with a scorned Jarvis and her determined father, but I'd just be observing from the sidelines. I couldn't afford to do anything more.

CHAPTER FOUR

Jolie

IT WAS my first full day back at the lab and I was nervous. Only because I was worried that I would have to field a thousand questions about my non-wedding. I'd sent cards to every single guest, apologizing and making arrangements to return all the gifts, but I was still dealing with the fallout.

"Welcome back." Corrine Chao, another one of the grad students in the lab, greeted me with a warm smile.

"Thanks." I locked my purse in my desk drawer as I booted up my laptop.

"You okay?" she asked softly. "I think what you did was really brave."

I lifted one shoulder in a halfhearted shrug. "I don't know what I am right now but thank you. I probably could have handled it a dozen other ways, you know?"

"You did what you had to. My mother's been divorced four times—I think she wishes she'd backed out. At least with the last two."

"We all have twenty-twenty vision in hindsight. I just got lucky because I happened to overhear him saying something at the rehearsal dinner that got me thinking. By the time I got to the church, I knew I couldn't do it." I really hadn't wanted to talk about this today, but Corrine was a friend. And she'd been one of the people I'd left sitting at the church. I felt like I owed her at least a small explanation.

"Honestly, I always wondered what you saw in him. He's good-looking, I guess, but he was always so full of himself. Obviously, I didn't spend a lot of time with him, so I didn't think it was my place to say anything. He seemed like a real narcissist, and I couldn't figure out what you saw in him."

"It was all set up by my dad and I allowed myself to get swept up in it."

"Well, at least you came to your senses before you had kids or anything."

I shuddered. "I totally dodged that bullet."

We grinned at each other before a familiar voice spoke behind me.

"Look who it is. Everyone's favorite runaway bride." Ellen Hayes-Camalleri, PhD. was a ballbuster and a half. She didn't like me and I couldn't stand her, but we'd found a way to coexist over the last couple of years. While she already had her doctorate, she'd been working eighty-hour weeks to publish the results of her work, hoping to someday be running her own lab somewhere like Harvard or MIT. And she drove me crazy on a daily basis.

I'd hated having to invite her to the wedding, but it would have been a huge insult not to. Now I was probably never going to hear the end of it.

"Dr. Camalleri, you have a phone call!" someone called out from the other side of the room.

"Saved by the bell," Corrine whispered as Dr. Camalleri headed in the other direction.

"I'm sure she'll find me," I murmured.

"I'll come up with a question or five," Corrine said, winking. "Don't worry. I've got your back."

"Thanks. I totally owe you a drink."

"And I will collect."

I turned to my computer and opened my email. As expected, the DNA sequences were ready and waiting. A series of clicks opened a file and my heart dropped. In front of me was a hot mess, much like my life. Back to step one. There was no moving forward without knowing the exact locations of transgene insertion. With a heavy sigh, I stood up. Back to the tissue culture room to start again.

Usually, it was easy to immerse myself in work, but my head was all over the place today. Instead of focusing on tissue cultures, I kept thinking about my wedding dress, of all things. How much I'd loved it and how it was now in its storage bag in the back of the closet of my old room at my parents' house. How I'd probably never wear it again. How I hadn't had a chance to talk to the friends and family who'd come in from out of town. The lobster dinner I'd never gotten to enjoy. The honeymoon I wasn't on.

It wasn't about Jarvis. I couldn't care less if I ever saw him again. But I'd missed out on everything a wedding day was supposed to be, and while he wasn't the man I was supposed to be with, I couldn't help but wonder if I'd ever have this chance again. Even if I eventually met someone special, I couldn't expect my parents to put on another wedding, and with a future in academia, I most likely wouldn't have the money either.

Okay, knock it off.

I spoke sternly to myself. It wasn't like me to get melancholy, and I had a lot of work to do. Even though I'd only taken off a few days instead of the full week I'd planned, I wanted to finish my studies and get my PhD. Until it was official, most things in my life would have to wait.

———

I WAS a few minutes late to the rink that night, and I skidded onto the ice as my dad and the other volunteers were taking roll. Johanna, a seven-year-old girl who wore her hair in a thick braid down her back, came stumbling over to me.

"I wanna be the goalie tonight," she announced.

Yesterday, she'd been all about playing defense.

"You can't just be the goalie," I told her gently, squatting down so we were eye level. "You don't have the right equipment."

Her mouth pulled into a pout. "But you said we could be anything we wanted to be if we worked hard."

"And I meant it. But being a goalie is different because of the equipment. You have to tell us ahead of time so we can find the right pieces in your size."

"It's not fair!" She stomped her foot and promptly wiped out. The group of kids standing around her laughed and her face turned red.

"Okay, that's enough," I warned the other kids before turning to her and holding out my hand.

"Come on, Johanna. We can talk more about the goalie thing, but not if you have a tantrum."

She sighed far more dramatically than the situation warranted but then reached up and took my hand so I could help her up.

"Tell you what," I said, once we'd split off to run drills with the different age groups. "If you work really hard on defense next week, I'll see if I can find goalie equipment in your size that you can try out."

"Yay!" Her eyes lit up as she followed the other kids as they warmed up.

None of the kids in her age group had wanted to be a goalie this session, but I honestly didn't believe we had anything that would fit her, so that wound up being a good thing. This camp for underprivileged children in the St. Louis area was ongoing, running a few days a week during different times of the year. It took a ton of time for Dad to organize it, which was why he always enlisted the help of his players and anyone else willing to jump in.

Ironically, even though he treated Jarvis like a son, Jarvis had never volunteered. Not even in the off-season.

Looking around, it didn't escape me that both Nash Reilly and Michael Boone volunteered often, and tonight I'd spotted two other guys from the Mavericks, Lars Jansson and Sawyer Cain, in the locker room helping the youngest boys learn how to put on their equipment.

Lars had a pregnant wife at home, but he still found the time to help.

Jarvis had no excuses and he'd never shown up in all the years Dad had been doing it.

I couldn't believe I'd almost married him.

"Coach Jolie," a little girl named Bethany tugged on my pants. "I have to go potty."

"Can you go by yourself, or do you need me to help you?"

She wiggled nervously. "I can't get my equipment off."

I looked around to see who was nearby and motioned to Michael, who skated over to me.

"What's up?"

"Can you watch my group for a few minutes? I have to take Bethany to the bathroom."

"Sure." He nodded, probably glad none of his players had to go.

I helped Bethany get half-undressed and then helped her put everything back on once she'd done her business. It took nearly fifteen minutes and by the time we got back on the ice, Boone had my group of girls doing a skating drill with his boys. And it was a clusterfuck. The boys were mostly faster but in many cases clumsier. The girls had a lot of heart but took it harder when they lost the individual heats.

"Thank god," Michael breathed when he saw me. "I thought you'd made another run for it."

"Nice." My voice dripped with sarcasm.

"I was just kidding."

"Whatever." I blew my whistle, motioning to the girls.

"Jolie. Hey." Michael skated alongside me. "I was really only trying to be funny. While you were gone, two of the girls started to cry and one of the boys announced he didn't think girls should play hockey."

"I love kids, but no one ever said coaching them was easy."

He snickered as I skated away.

I rounded up the girls and gave them a little pep talk before letting them practice shooting into the net. Without a goalie, they didn't have any barriers, but most of them didn't have good aim anyway.

"Hey, Jolie, you coming out with us after this?" Jana, the only other female coach at the camp right now, called out to me as we changed in the women's locker room. My feet still hadn't adjusted to being on skates again and I was so glad to take them off.

"Where are you going?" I asked curiously, massaging the ball of my foot.

"Over to Harley's for wings and whatever." She

leaned over and lowered her voice. "Michael Boone is going. Is he gorgeous or what?" She had a dreamy look on her face and I nearly rolled my eyes.

"I guess he's all right. Personally, I'm done with hockey players. He's all yours."

"But are you coming?"

"I don't know. I have to be at my lab in the morning."

"There's never a better time to get back on the horse, you know?" She gave me a serious look.

Jeez. Did everyone know about my freakin' wedding disaster?

Well, I certainly wasn't going to talk about it to someone I'd only known for three days.

"Who else is going?" I asked instead.

"I think the whole volunteer staff from the camp and some of their significant others. There's about twelve of us so far."

"Let me think about it," was all I said.

I rarely went out, but I was hungry. It couldn't hurt to have a beer, some chicken wings and hang out with the other volunteers.

"Is my dad going?" I asked suddenly.

"Oh. No, he said he had to go home."

Thank god.

The last thing I wanted to do was hang out with my dad right now. If I had to listen to him tell me how much Jarvis missed me one more time, I might vomit.

I probably should have gone home too, but the rumbling in my stomach reminded me there wasn't much in the way of groceries there. And I was starving after all the skating I'd done tonight.

"I guess I can go for one beer," I said at last.

"Awesome! You can be my wingman." She paused. "Wing-girl. Wing-person?"

"You'll probably be sorely disappointed in my wing-person skills," I said, chuckling.

"Can't be worse than my flirting skills."

Yeah, it could.

CHAPTER FIVE

Boone

"You're looking better every day, man," I told my teammate Sawyer on our drive to Harley's. "Saw you smoking those seven-year-olds on skating drills."

"Fuck you," he said smoothly. "It's not easy coming back when you become one with your couch for as long as I did."

Sawyer was in a bad place following his wife's death—drinking so much we'd had to hold a minor interventionbut he'd finally pulled himself back up and reentered the land of the living. He was practicing and traveling with the team again but hadn't returned to games yet.

"We're gonna put that little guy Teddy in goal at

the next youth practice and let you take some shots," Nash said to Sawyer.

"The five-year-old?" I furrowed my brow. "I don't know if Sawyer's ready for that, man."

Nash shrugged. "Well, it'll either build Sawyer's confidence or Teddy's."

From the passenger seat, Sawyer held up both middle fingers, making sure Nash saw them from the driver's seat and I saw them from the back seat. It was damn good to see some life in him again, and I knew he'd be back in fighting form soon. In the meantime, we made fun of him because that was what teammates did.

"Speaking of confidence," Nash said, meeting my gaze in the rearview mirror, "you've got nads of steel talking to Gizzard's daughter so much."

"It wasn't that much," I said.

Sawyer scoffed. "I've never even made eye contact with her, dude. And I never will."

"It's not her fault her dad's an overbearing asshole," I said. "I'm not going to ignore her."

"I still can't believe you picked her up in the church parking lot," Nash said. "Does Coach know about that yet?"

"I think Jolie told him. She said she didn't really give me a choice."

"Is that the truth?" Nash asked, his tone skeptical.

"Yeah, it was either drive away and risk running over her foot or let her in the car."

"I'm not sure which way I would've gone on that," Nash said.

He pulled his new Escalade into the parking lot of Harley's and found a spot. We were walking toward the front door when Sawyer gave me a serious look.

"Hey, how's your brother doing?" he asked.

He asked about Andy regularly. Sawyer had lost his wife Annie to cancer, and I felt like he understood its toll better than my other teammates.

"Hanging in there," I said. "He's really sick from the chemo."

"It's a bitch."

"It's hard for him that his wife has to take care of everything."

Sawyer nodded. "For better or worse, though. This is definitely the worst."

We dropped the subject when we walked inside and saw a table of other coaches from youth hockey. Gizzard and several Mavericks players coached when we were able to with our schedule, and there were others who did the same. It was never the same group twice.

Nash's girlfriend Sariah had saved seats for us,

and he kissed her on the cheek as he slid into the seat next to hers.

"The cheek?" I gave Sariah a thumbs-down. "You want me to show you how a real man greets his girl?"

Nash scoffed. "Like you'd know. You haven't had a girlfriend since *fetch* was a thing."

"Stop trying to make *fetch* happen," Sariah said. "It's not going to happen."

"Exactly my point." Nash grinned.

Jolie made a little bowing motion to Sariah with her arms from the other side of the table.

"You got your guy to use *Mean Girls* references correctly. I bow down to you."

Sariah gave her a triumphant look. "We take turns picking the movie for movie night."

"What did you pick on your last night?" I asked Nash.

He grinned at Sariah. "Babe?"

Sariah's expression turned serious as she said, "Leave the gun. Take the cannoli."

"*The Godfather*," I said approvingly. "A true classic."

Nash put his arm around Sariah and kissed her temple. He'd been the last of my teammates I expected to settle down, but he'd found someone perfect for him, and I often found myself wishing I had what he did.

Not Sariah, of course, but someone of my own I could have inside jokes and movie nights with. Someone who would save me seats and remind me my mom's birthday was coming up.

It was next to impossible, though, when I never knew if women liked me for myself or for being a professional athlete with a professional athlete's salary. The few times I'd had girlfriends since getting drafted, they'd wanted to be seen with me, and they'd agreed with everything I said or did like I was incapable of being wrong. Even Missy, the girlfriend I'd proposed to last year, had been more excited about my job than me. She'd turned me down, which, in retrospect, was the right call.

I wanted someone like my teammate Wes's wife, Hadley, who was his best friend and fiercest ally, but also the first one to call him out on his bullshit.

"Is your girlfriend coming tonight, Michael?" one of the female volunteer coaches asked me.

"Oh, it's Boone, and I'm single," I said.

Nash put a hand next to his mouth like he was about to tell her a secret, and then he loudly announced, "He was born without a nut sac. It's just a little tiny flap of skin."

I shook my head. "You're so full of shit."

The woman looked back and forth between us like she wasn't sure who to believe.

"He's got balls," Sawyer said, settling it. "I mean, technically. He's still a pussy."

Her face lit up and she laughed. "Well, I'm Jana, and I loved the way you raced that group of boys at practice and let one of them win."

Sawyer and Nash exchanged a look and Sawyer said, "He was trying his best, Jana. That seven-year-old was just a beast."

Jesus, they were on a roll tonight. Jana's eyes widened like she was once again unsure whether he was telling the truth, but Jolie laughed beside her.

"Does anyone want to share wings with me?" she asked. "I can't eat a pound because I also want tots, but there's a special, so I should order the pound."

I studied her for a couple of seconds as the server set a mug of beer in front of her. A woman who wasn't afraid to throw down some beer and wings? Now *that* was hot.

"I'll share some with you," I said. "I'm starving, so let's get two pounds."

"What kind of sauce do you like?" she asked. "Or do you like rubs?"

Nash's expression was gleeful. "Does he like rubs? Let me tell"

"Give it a rest, asshole," I said, shoving his shoulder lightly.

"What?" He put his palms up, feigning innocence. "She set me up perfectly. I couldn't let that go."

"Ignore him," I said to Jolie. "I'll eat any of the sauces except that mango one."

"Hmm…" She scanned the menu. "How much spice can you handle?"

I glared at Nash. "Don't even think about it."

Jolie laughed, the sound light and genuinely amused. "Are you guys like this all the time?"

I shrugged. "I know he doesn't look very deep, but Nash has many sides. Sometimes he's an asshole, but he can also be a complete dick. And other times, he's a douchebag."

Sariah met Jolie's gaze across the table. "Yes, they're like this all the time."

"I guess I've only seen them on their best behavior when my dad's around," Jolie said, giving me a quick look before adding, "but that's no fun."

She was confident, and I was intrigued by it. What if I'd also only seen her on her best behavior because her dad was around, other than the brief time we spent together when I'd given her a ride home from the church?

"Pick the spiciest sauce you like and that will

work for me," I said, focusing on our food order again.

"You like spicy?" she asked, arching her brows.

"Love it."

Her small smile spread into a full grin. "Me too. Let's get the reaper."

Nash groaned, and I knew why. He'd ordered the hottest wing sauce on a road trip recently and paid the price afterward.

"Hope you guys are in the mood for a colon cleanse," he said.

"My colon is made of steel," I assured him.

"Same," Jolie said. "Your colon must be delicate, Nash."

Sawyer reached across the table to high-five her, saying, "First burn, well done."

"Are there vegan options on this menu?" Jana asked, looking at the back of it.

"Are tots vegan?" Jolie asked.

Jana gave her a withering look, and Jolie tried to suppress a smile. I watched her as everyone else talked, looking at someone else every once in a while. No guy wanted to be labeled a creeper.

When she took her stocking cap off and shook out her hair, I had to shift in my seat because I started to get hard. There was something sexy about seeing her thick, red waves spilling over her shoulders. I imagined that was what she looked like in the morning, fresh out of bed.

The food came, and I checked the text that had just come in on my phone.

Nash: Stop staring at her. Coach will neuter you if you sleep with his daughter.

Shit. If he'd noticed, others might, too. I couldn't risk anything getting back to Coach, so I forced my attention to my food.

The wing sauce was legit, and though I loved it, just a few bites had my eyes watering. I wiped the corner of one with a napkin and snuck a glance at Jolie.

"I love this sauce," she said. "You like it?"

"Yeah, it's good."

It was good, but *fuck* was it hot. I'd finished my beer and my own water and our server hadn't returned to the table, so I grabbed Sawyer's untouched water and downed half of it.

"So Jolie, what do you do?" Sariah asked.

"I'm still in school. Grad school, studying micro-biology."

Nash gave me an enthusiastic look. "Did you hear that, Boone? She's got a microscope. If you're nice to her, you might be able to borrow it and finally get a look at your peen."

"Shit, Nash," I said, laughing as I finished a wing.

"You'd think you were on stage doing a comedy routine tonight."

"Microbiology sounds interesting," Sariah said, ignoring us.

Jolie nodded. "I think so."

"What are you hoping to do when you're done with school?" Sariah asked.

"I'd like to teach."

"You'd be good at that," Nash said, making his first serious comment of the night. "You're good with the kids in the youth hockey group."

"Thanks. I used to babysit a lot. I wanted brothers and sisters so bad, but I'm an only child."

Sawyer cringed. "I can't imagine being Coach Gizzard's only child. He can be pretty intense."

"He's a lot different at home," Jolie said. "Hockey is what he gets most intense about. I didn't always care for it when I was the one playing, but now we can sort of bond over it. I always say I need to have a defibrillator on hand when I watch games on TV with him."

I could just imagine Giz yelling at players on the screen the same way he laid into us in the locker room. I admired his intensity, though.

"You get to watch him riding our asses instead of him riding yours," I cracked.

"Exactly." She grinned and reached for another wing.

"How has your dad been about you calling off your wedding?" Sariah asked. "Or is that not something you want to talk about?"

"No, I don't mind talking about it. He's still convinced I'm hormonal or something. My mom has pretty much come around, so my dad will eventually."

Sariah gave Jolie a sympathetic look. "Good. If it wasn't right for you, you definitely made the right call."

"Your gift is on the way back to you," Jolie assured her.

Sariah waved a hand. "Who cares about the gift? What matters is that you're okay."

"I appreciate that," Jolie said. "I'm great."

After another beer and more conversation, she took out her wallet and reached for some cash.

"No, I've got it," I said, putting a palm up.

"No, take this."

She offered me thirty dollars.

"No, seriously, I've got it. I'm sure we'll all go out again and you can get me back if you want."

She looked wary but then put the money away, saying, "Okay, thanks."

I wasn't going to let her pay next time, but I

knew it was the only way she'd let me pick up the check this time. And even though I wanted to offer her a ride home and maybe get an invite back to her place, I kept my mouth shut.

It was a risk I couldn't take. Whatever the hell *fetch* was, Jolie and I were like that.

Never going to happen.

CHAPTER SIX

Jolie

GRANDMA G and I had started our monthly lunch dates when I was young. Back when my grandfather was alive and she'd still been driving. Until I was around twelve, our lunch dates consisted of an early movie and a late lunch, and we'd alternate who got to pick the movie. As I moved into my teens, we'd sometimes substitute shopping for the movie, and once she even went roller-skating with me and my friends.

She'd slowed down a lot in the last five or six years, but I still enjoyed the hell out of our time together.

I hadn't thought we'd get together this month

because of the wedding and everything else, but when she'd called yesterday, I'd been happy to make time for her. She waved as I pulled up to the front of the building she lived in and she hopped into my Jeep like she owned it.

"Hi." She leaned over and kissed my cheek.

"I love that scarf," I told her, referring to the long, red-and-purple scarf with an abstract design.

"Thank you. Your father brought it back for me from Iceland when he and your mother went a couple of years ago."

"I didn't even get a gift from that trip," I said, laughing as I put the Jeep in gear.

"Well, I guess we know who your dad's favorite mom is," she quipped.

"No doubt about that."

"How are you doing, sweetie?"

"I'm good. Better than I thought I'd be."

"Has your father settled down at all after the Jarvis fiasco?"

"Yes and no. He's not angry anymore, but he's still pushing Jarvis on me like an old coat."

"And Jarvis?"

"He calls and texts and yesterday sent me a huge gift basket from Hotel Chocolat." Anyone that knew me was aware they were my favorite gourmet chocolates.

"Ah. Your weakness."

"Not if they come from him. I gave the chocolate away to the kids at the hockey camp last night."

She snickered. "I do love you, my dear Jolie."

I glanced over at her. "Is that sarcasm?"

"Not at all."

"I've told him to stop, that there's no hope of reconciliation, but Dad is driving this. No doubt."

"You're truly over him?"

"Grandma, I was never in love with him. I liked him, and it was exciting for a while, but I walked away from our wedding without looking back. And unless he calls or texts, I don't even think about him. My only regret is how much money was wasted."

She reached over and patted my leg. "Then it's time to move on. Any prospects?"

For some reason, Boone's incredibly blue eyes came to mind, and I quickly forced the image away. "Nope. Not interested. I'm focused on my PhD. There will be plenty of time for dating once that's done."

"What about sex?"

I didn't bother hiding my laughter. "You're a little too interested in my sex life."

"Because I don't want you to waste your time with any more selfish men. You deserve better."

"Was, uh, Grandpa selfish?" I couldn't believe I

was asking and practically held my breath as I waited for her response.

She just smiled, though. "At first. But I figured it out and we had a talk."

Figures my grandmother would have been a trailblazer in the sex-talk-with-your-husband department.

"That's good." What else could I say?

"Don't let your father—or anyone else—bully you into doing things you don't want to do. You're a smart, strong woman, but I saw this coming a mile away. Wait for a man who deserves you, Jolie."

"Believe me, that's the plan. It's just, you know, tall redheaded biologists with big hips aren't exactly at the top of most men's dating list."

"Stop that." She gave me a look even though I could only see it in my peripheral vision. "You're stunning. It's just going to take the right guy to see that your beauty goes deeper than what's on the outside. And anyway, those long legs of yours? Most men would kill to see them in a short skirt and high heels."

"Yeah, but most men aren't tall enough for a woman like me to wear heels."

"Insecure men. A real man will love having a taller woman on his arm. Trust me on this. Where do you think you got your height?"

I smiled at the idea of my grandmother walking around in a miniskirt and stilettos. It had probably happened in the sixties and seventies.

"I just want someone who appreciates all of me," I said slowly. "I don't need another scientist who understands my work—that's not a thing. But he has to get *me*, the woman beneath the nerdy science stuff."

"There's nothing nerdy about being a scientist. You're working on something that could impact the future of the medical community. You know how many blind people could potentially benefit from your research?"

"That's why I do it, but Jarvis actually asked me what the retina was and why anyone would care that I was focusing my dissertation on something to do with it."

"He's a schmuck."

I laughed. "He is."

"You know, your dad has some very handsome single men on the Mavericks. Have you ever thought about any of them?"

Like Michael Boone?

Yeah, no.

"Nope. That's a hard line for Dad and I don't blame him. How embarrassing would it be if I was sleeping with his players and guys were talking about me in the locker room?" I shuddered at the thought.

"Did I say anything about multiple players? What about that nice Sawyer Cain? He's a widower now."

"Grandma, stop." I pulled into a parking space at the restaurant and looked at her. "I'll find someone when I'm ready. It's not now."

At least, that was the plan.

———

I WAS LATE GETTING to my lab in the morning and of course, my father called me as I was walking into the building.

"Hi, Dad. I'm running late—is everything okay?"

"Yeah, it's fine." His gruff voice always made me smile, even when he drove me crazy. "I just wanted to talk for a few minutes."

"Well, I've got about three minutes until I get upstairs."

"Jarvis called. He said you haven't thanked him for the chocolate."

Ah, there it was.

I'd been expecting it, but enough was enough already.

"Daddy, I love you, but you have to stop," I said quietly. "It's over. Do you really think I want to be with a man who doesn't find me attractive? Is that what you want for me? Is that how you feel about Mom?"

Dad was quiet for a long time, and I stopped walking, waiting for his response because I didn't want to have this conversation in the lab.

"Sweetheart, I just want to be sure you marry someone who'll take care of you. You're so lost in that lab of yours most of the time, you'll be one of those old ladies with nothing but books and four hundred cats."

"I'm allergic to cats, so we're safe from that scenario."

He sighed. "Has anyone ever told you how stubborn you are?"

"I wonder where that comes from?" I countered.

"You do have a point."

"Look, I'm already late. I have to go. See you at dinner on Sunday. Love you." I quickly disconnected the call and took the stairs two at a time.

"Morning!" Corrine gave me a grin.

How was she always so happy?

"Look who it is." Ellen glanced at her watch. "Only fourteen minutes late."

"I was here until midnight last night," I said, yanking on my lab coat.

"How else are you going to finish your dissertation?"

I ignored her as I booted up my computer and opened my email.

Crap.

Once again, the results weren't what I'd been hoping for, which meant starting this part over. Again.

"No good?" Corrine asked sympathetically, looking over at me.

"Nope. Dammit, why does this keep happening?"

"Maybe if you had your mind on science instead of boys, you'd have better results." Ellen's voice made me want to throw something at her.

"My mind is right where it needs to be," I muttered.

"Trust me," she said, perching on the edge of my desk. "You're better off without a man. They're nothing but trouble. And obviously, it's impacting your progress."

"I just broke off an engagement," I said, trying to keep the irritation out of my voice. "It's only natural to take a few weeks to grieve, get past it."

"Well, that's fine, but you'll only have yourself to blame when your research goes to shit." She walked away chuckling and I shot her the bird. From under my desk where no one could see it.

We'd butted heads from the start. She wasn't in charge of my project, but she was tight with our PI, the primary investigator who ran the lab. Dr. Archie Matello could derail my academic career if I wasn't careful, and Ellen was his handpicked protégé.

"Ignore her," Corrine said. "She just needs to get laid."

"Don't we all?"

She giggled. "Not me. This guy I'm seeing is freakin' amazing. He works in the physics lab and I have to say, I highly recommend dating a nerd. They've spent their whole lives thinking about sex, so when they finally get some, all they care about is pleasing you." She fanned herself dramatically.

"Do you ever think about anything but sex?" I teased.

She squinted. "Is that a trick question? Don't you think about sex?"

"Well, sure, but not constantly."

"Danny and I had a one-night stand a few months ago that rocked my world. I think he ruined me for all other men because it was so good, but I didn't think he was my type. Then we ran into each other on campus and I decided to give him a chance. And you know what? Once you get past the nerdy exterior, there's a lot of sexy man beneath."

"I'll bet." I'd met Danny a few times and he

seemed nice enough, but I didn't get sexy vibes from him. Of course, what did I know? Jarvis had a pretty sexy exterior and had turned out to be a dud both on the inside and in the bedroom.

I wanted to ask her what, exactly, Danny brought to the table that was so awesome, but that wasn't a conversation to have here or now. Not with Ellen and Dr. Matello both in the lab today.

I'd give it some thought later, though.

After the conversation with my grandmother, I had to admit I wanted and deserved someone who'd give me everything I needed, both physically and emotionally. I didn't know exactly what that was, though, which was why dating was on the back burner until after I had my PhD.

Being in a relationship felt like so much work, and I already had my hands full trying to finish my dissertation and stay in Dr. Matello's good graces.

Sex and romance would have to wait.

CHAPTER SEVEN

Boone

MAVERICKS GROUP TEXT

Lars: Sheridan is crying because we are out of cookies and the bakery is closed.

Drew: Avoid eye contact and apologize. It's the only response when your pregnant wife is crying.

Lars: I offered to go get cookies from the grocery store and she told me to go fuck myself.

Wes: Pregnant women are always right. You should definitely GFY.

Lars: I don't know if I can survive the rest of this pregnancy. Can we leave early for our road trip?

Kon: You didn't hear? The road trip is canceled.

Lars: What? How? Why?

Wes: He's kidding.

Boone: You can always come coach youth hockey. It starts in 2 hours.

Lars: No, I told Sheridan we could spend time together before I leave tomorrow.

Nash: Enjoy, bro!

Lars: I hate you all.

I WAS in the middle of packing for my road trip to Calgary when my phone screen lit up from its spot on my bed beside my open suitcase. When I saw my agent's name, Evelyn, on the caller ID, I dropped the T-shirt I'd been folding and lunged for the phone.

She was feeling out the possibility of a trade to Nashville, keeping it as low-key as possible for now. With the Mavericks in playoff contention, it wasn't an ideal time to be asking for a move. Nothing mattered to me but being with my brother, though, so I was willing to ask, bargain, or even beg if it got me back home to him.

"Hey, Evelyn," I said, my heart racing. "What's up?"

"First things first—how's Andy?"

She was a no-nonsense woman in her midforties

with a reputation as a hard-ass. And when she was working on behalf of her clients, she was one. But Evelyn also had a big heart. She always remembered the names of my family members and remembered to ask about them. She always sent thoughtful gifts to mark my career milestones. Compared to some of my teammates, who couldn't always get calls to their agents returned, I was fortunate.

"He's okay," I said, sitting down on the brown leather chair in the corner of my bedroom. "This round of chemo is making him really sick, but the doctors said that would happen. I'm waiting on my sister-in-law to call me back when we can talk alone, so I can find out if he's telling me everything or not."

She hummed with concern. "You think he's not telling you everything?"

"I don't know. He's so worried about me staying focused on hockey and not worrying about him, I wouldn't put it past him to put on a strong front."

"I hope not."

I sighed heavily. "Me too. This is already a shit-covered sundae covered with shit sauce and shit sprinkles. I'm not sure I can take a giant turd on top."

"I can always count on you to be eloquent," Evelyn cracked.

"Just keeping it real."

"And I like that about you," she said. "You know I

always keep it real, too. The prospects for a trade to Nashville aren't looking great."

"Fuck."

"I'm sorry. You know how hockey is. One injury could change everything out of nowhere. They know we're interested, so now it's going to be a waiting game."

"Waiting takes time," I said, my elbows on my knees. "And I don't know that I have time."

"They're in playoff contention, too, and they don't want to make any big changes right now."

I rubbed my forehead, wishing I had the freedom to move just because I wanted to. Being locked up in a contract wasn't everything people thought it was.

"I'll take a pay cut," I told my agent. "I don't care which line I play on. Just get me there, Evelyn. Please."

"I'll do my best. I promise you that."

I stood up, stress pushing on my chest like a weight.

"I know you will," I said. "Just let me know if anything develops. Anything at all."

———

"CAN WE PRACTICE FIGHTING?" a kid named Trevor asked me as we waited for everyone to get on the ice for youth practice that evening.

When I skated onto the ice for a game, I had to be focused. Even though I was just here to help coach these kids tonight, I'd still felt lighter as soon as I'd skated onto the ice. It was embedded in me; the ice was a safe place.

"Yeah, we can start with you against me," I said to Trevor. "What do you think?"

He lowered his brows. "I meant another kid, Mr. Boone. You can't fight me."

"I could." I rubbed my chin like I was considering it. "I need to practice breaking noses, and yours is so perfect."

Trevor was a bruiser; he was one of my favorite kids here. We didn't let the kids fight, ever, but he still asked.

"That's child abuse," he said. "You'd go to jail."

I ruffled his hair. "I'm not gonna fight you, kid, relax. You're here to learn hockey fundamentals and that's it."

He groaned with annoyance. "That's boring."

"Hey, Coach!" I called out to Gizzard, who was setting up orange cones for a drill.

He looked over at me.

"We've got a kid here who thinks practice is

boring."

Coach furrowed his brow, looking concerned. "Well, we can't have that, can we? What might be fun for him?"

"He wants to fight," I said.

Coach nodded. "Well, show him what I have you guys do when you want to fight."

Trevor looked up at me, his eyes bright and hopeful. "We get to fight?"

"No, something way more fun," I assured him. "It's called a bag skate. You're going to love it."

———

IT ONLY TOOK thirty minutes of nonstop skating with me blowing a whistle behind him for Trevor to decide that practicing with the other kids didn't sound so bad after all.

Jolie was working with a group of kids on shooting when Joey and I skated over to join them.

"He'll sleep well tonight," she said.

"Yeah, he did pretty well, though. For an eight-year-old." We exchanged a look as we stood back and watched the line of kids take shots. "Did your dad ever coach you?"

She laughed. "Oh yeah. He *volunteered*"—she air-quoted the word—"to help coach my peewee team, but he didn't even wait to see if the head coach wanted his help."

"The old bulldozer routine?" I quipped.

"Yep. You would've thought we were training for the Olympics."

Tonight, she wore a purple knitted ear warmer and a Mavericks team fleece. Again, she looked right at home on the ice, and again, I felt a pull toward her.

"Did you like it?" I asked her. "Having your dad help coach?"

She shrugged. "When I was younger, I loved it. But as I got older, we worked out an agreement where he could watch my practices and come to my games, but he couldn't come coach me during games."

I nodded, easily able to picture Coach steam-rolling an inexperienced coach. "Yeah, I imagine that was for the best."

Coach called everyone together and announced we were going to play a game, and the kids cheered with glee. Games were always a disaster at youth practices, but this was a beginner-level group, and Coach Gizzard wanted the kids to have some fun with it and hopefully, get enthusiastic about playing more seriously for a competitive youth hockey team.

Volunteers played on the teams to help guide the

kids, and I found myself on offense against Jolie. She was good, smoothly passing the puck to the kids and telling them when to pass and when to shoot.

I'd always thought she was beautiful. Getting to know her a little had changed the way I saw her, though. She was easygoing and secure in who she was. Her smile drew me in and made it hard to look away.

She was more off-limits than ever, but I was more interested than ever. That was a dangerous combination. Nash wasn't here tonight to remind me not to stare, and that's exactly what I was doing when Jolie helped a kid shoot a puck right past me and into the net.

When she grinned at me, obviously thinking I'd let him score on purpose, I smiled back.

"Boone!" Coach yelled, snapping me out of my trance. "We need you on the bench."

Shit. He'd busted me staring at Jolie. That was the last thing I needed.

I went to the bench, where two kids needed help lacing their skates and another needed help going to the bathroom.

"I don't know how to wipe," the kid said once he was in the stall.

Taking kids to the bathroom was enough; I drew the line at wiping asses.

"Want me to go get your mom?" I asked.

"It's the boys' room. She can't come in here."

"We'll make an exception," I said. "I'll be right back. What's your name?"

"Camden."

I went to the stands and asked for Camden's mom until I found her, and once she was in the bathroom with him, I checked my phone and saw a missed call from Carrie. There was also a text.

Carrie: I'm free for the next 40 minutes if you want to call.

I CHECKED my watch and saw that I still had fifteen minutes left, so I pushed the call back button immediately. Since Andy's diagnosis, I'd checked in with her like this several times to find out how things were really going.

"Hey," she said. "How are you?"

"I'm good. How are you guys?"

"We—hang on, I'm putting stuff on the conveyor belt at the grocery store...okay, we're okay. You know, some days are better than others, but overall, we're okay."

"Do you need to call me back?"

"No, I just have a handful of things. I can talk to you while I check out."

"Is Andy still getting sick from the chemo?"

"Reliably. It weakens him a lot and he feels bad about spending so much time in bed, even though I keep telling him that he needs to rest."

I closed my eyes, the image of my strong brother brought to his knees turning my stomach.

"Do the doctors have any idea if the treatment is working?" I asked.

"Not yet. He'll get scans after this round of treatment." Her voice got faint as she covered the phone. "Thanks so much. Have a good night."

"Is the wait hard as hell for you?" I asked her.

"It's really hard, yeah. But I go to counseling every week, and my counselor tells me to take it one day at a time. That's all I can do. So I try to keep busy. You can't lie awake worrying when you fall asleep the moment your head hits the pillow."

I sat down on a wood bench. "I'm doing what I can to get there. And I'd really appreciate it if you'd let me send you some money."

"Let's not go there. I promised Andy I wouldn't do anything behind his back, and I keep my word to my husband."

I moved the phone away from my mouth so I could breathe out my frustration.

"We're okay, Michael."

Only my family called me that, and it hit me right in the chest.

"Promise me you'll let me know if anything changes or you get the results of the scans," I said.

"I promise. I'm taking good care of him."

"I know you are, Carrie. I'm…" I cleared the emotion from my throat. "I'm proud of you. And I love you guys."

"Love you, too. Win that next game for us, okay?"

I smiled. My brother and I had grown up playing hockey together, and he was my biggest supporter.

"I will," I said.

CHAPTER EIGHT

Jolie

I POURED my third cup of coffee of the morning, hoping it would help me wake up a little. I'd been working long hours at the lab, I was at the rink almost every night trying to get back in my father's good graces, and sometimes I came back to the lab after I left there. I'd been burning the candle at both ends the last couple of weeks and it was catching up to me.

On top of how busy I was, sleep seemed to be elusive lately too.

I'd get into bed, my eyes would get heavy, and then I simply couldn't fall asleep. I'd toss and turn before eventually getting up and reading for a while.

By the time I fell asleep, it was usually three or four in the morning, and I was always up by seven.

Tonight I was going to go to the rink for a couple of hours, make sure I was out of there by eight, and head home. I'd run a hot bath, pour a glass of wine, and read a few chapters of the book that had been sitting untouched on my nightstand for months. Hopefully, I'd be asleep by ten.

"You going to the hockey camp again tonight?" Corrine asked me as I started gathering my things at five thirty.

"Yeah, it's been good to get some exercise."

"I need to make time for exercise."

I heard a snort coming from Ellen's direction, but I didn't have time to get into it with her today.

Instead, I smiled at Corrine. "See you tomorrow. And don't forget we're going to lunch for Dr. M's birthday."

"See you then."

I took the stairs down to the exit and walked out to the parking lot. I'd already changed into sweats, a long-sleeved turtleneck, and a well-worn Mavericks hoodie, so I was warm even though it was cold out. The heat in the Jeep had been wonky lately and my gut told me I'd need a new car sooner rather than later. I'd been doing everything I could to avoid that since I didn't want to have to ask my parents for money, but I didn't know how I'd swing it otherwise.

Luckily, the heat came on after a couple of minutes and I turned up the radio, singing along to Taylor Swift.

I was almost to the rink when a weird yellow light flashed on the dashboard.

Fuck.

What the hell was that?

I knew it wasn't the check engine light, but I didn't pay all that much attention. If something was wrong, I'd ask my dad or take it to the mechanic he used. Dad tended to tinker with the Jeep in the off-season, making sure my tires didn't need replacing and that I'd kept up with oil changes. It was stuff I probably should have been doing myself, but I'd always been focused on school and Dad either did it or paid someone else to take care of it. I'd assumed Jarvis would take over car maintenance once we were married, and part of me was embarrassed to admit I'd been okay with letting a man handle anything to do with the vehicle I drove.

Why couldn't I handle it? I was perfectly capable.

A weird thumping sound made my heart skip a beat and I unconsciously slowed down.

Did I have a flat? Was that what the stupid light had been? It had gone away after a couple of minutes, so I'd figured I'd be okay until I got to the rink.

Now I wasn't going to make it.

Son of a bitch.

I pulled onto the shoulder and put on my hazard lights.

Sure enough, the front right tire was flat.

I blew out a breath and put on my coat.

Dad had taught me how to change a tire before he'd allowed me to get my license. But that was the only time I'd ever done it. Nearly a decade ago.

I could call him.

Or I could pull up my big-girl pants and do some adulting.

I could do this.

How hard could it be?

I was a strong, capable, independent woman.

Yeah, right.

This was going to be a disaster.

―――――

I GOT to the rink an hour later looking like I'd just been in a fight. My hair was a mess, my hands, face, and clothes were covered in black dirt from the tire, and I'd broken two nails. I didn't worry about makeup or fancy clothes, but I tried not to look homeless when I was out in public.

"What happened to you?" Jana asked as I ran past the bench where she was handling the girls.

"Tell you in a minute!" I yelled back, making a beeline for the locker room.

I washed my hands and face, getting off most of the dirt and grime, and managed to run my fingers through my hair enough to get it into a ponytail. I looked rough, but there was no help for it, and I hurriedly laced up my skates.

"Sorry, everyone," I said as I got onto the ice. "I got a flat tire on the way here."

"And you changed it?" Jana's eyes widened. "That's awesome! I would've had to call my brother."

"Dad's busy with the team and I don't have any brothers," I retorted, feeling a little salty about the whole thing. I was proud of myself for managing to change the tire but irritated it had taken so long and had eventually required a cop to help me. It wasn't the tire changing that had been a problem, but I hadn't been strong enough to get the lug nuts off, so if the policeman hadn't shown up, I'd probably still be there.

"Coach Jolie! Coach Jolie! Look!" Johanna came waddling over to me wearing goalie gear, and

I couldn't help but grin at how cute she was.

"Well, look at you!" I reached out and gently tugged her braid. "Where did you get the equipment?"

"I dunno. It had my name on it when I got here."

I wondered if my father had been responsible for this? I'd mentioned Johanna a few times because I felt bad for her. Her father had been a Marine who'd been killed in a friendly fire incident overseas. Her mother had died in childbirth, so now her elderly great-grandparents were raising her. I didn't know anything beyond that, but I'd come to worry more about her than the others.

"Well, you better get out there and let Coach Kon show you a few moves. He doesn't come here very often."

Konstantin Volkov was the starting goalie for the Mavericks and he didn't volunteer very often. I'd heard it was because of the language barrier, but it seemed his English had gotten better this season.

I watched Johanna skate toward Kon on shaky feet, but I was proud of her. She'd probably be a great goalie once she got the hang of it. She was a tough little thing.

"Hey, you okay?" Boone's voice was soothing after the day I'd had, and I turned to him with a smile. Dad wasn't here tonight, so I didn't have to act like he had cooties.

"Hi. Yeah, just a flat tire. I handled it except for getting the stupid lug nuts off."

"They can be brutal," he agreed, his blue eyes meeting mine. "Make sure you don't drive on the donut too long—they're meant to be short-term fixes."

"I'll get a new tire tomorrow."

Hopefully. I had neither the time nor the money, but he didn't need to know that.

"If you need me to follow you home tonight, just in case, let me know."

"Thanks. I might take you up on that. It's supposed to snow again later."

"I'll find you once camp is over."

A tiny flutter of excitement raced through me.

He was soft-spoken and handsome, and I liked the way he interacted with the kids.

Not to mention those damn blue eyes.

Why was I thinking about this?

I didn't have time for men.

Did I?

Maybe just a little.

"Coach Jolie?" Johanna was tugging on the bottom of my hoodie, snapping me out of my thoughts.

"What's up, kiddo?"

She looked up at me from beneath her raised mask. "I don't think I like being goalie. Pucks *hurt*."

I managed not to laugh.

"I think you should give it more than fifteen minutes before you decide, okay? We'll try it for a couple of days. If you still don't like it, we'll move you back to defense. Is that fair?"

She contemplated it. "I guess so."

She pushed her mask back into place and skated toward the goal.

"Where do you find the patience?" Jana muttered under her breath. "I just want to give her a spanking."

"She lost her father last year and never knew her mother. Her great-grandparents, who are in their seventies, are raising her. I don't know what happened to both sets of grandparents, but she's had a rough time of it. I think we can find some extra patience for a seven-year-old who needs a little extra love."

Jana dipped her head. "You're right. That was a thoughtless thing to say."

"Don't get me wrong—there are times I want to strangle the whole bunch of them. But then I remember that most of these kids come from broken homes, single parents, stuff like that. That boy over there talking to Boone? He's going deaf and the parents don't have the money to pay for the surgery he needs. I'd like to think we can afford to give them some grace when they act like kids, since that's what they are."

"I didn't know that about Tommy." Jana followed my gaze.

"It's all right. Now, let's whip their butts into shape."

I grabbed a couple of extra sticks and blew my whistle.

Camp was over before I knew it and I couldn't wait to get home. I didn't want to think about new tires or the foot of snow we were supposed to get or anything but that bath waiting for me.

When I got out to the parking lot, Boone was standing by my car and I didn't like the look on his face.

"Houston, we have a problem," he said as I approached.

"Now what?" I asked in frustration.

"Your donut's flat."

I let out a string of curses as I stared at it.

"Do you have roadside assistance?" he asked.

"No," I grumbled. "I had it through my car insurance, but I let that feature lapse."

"Well, there's nothing you can do about the tire

tonight, but I can give you a ride home or wait with you while you call someone?"

"I…" There really wasn't anything that could be done tonight, and I could always call my mother in the morning. She'd help me figure it out. "You know, I'm going to take you up on the ride home. I'm done with this day and there's a bottle of wine with my name on it waiting for me."

"Then let's go. Do you need anything out of your car?"

"No, I've got my purse and laptop in here." I patted my backpack.

"Great. I can get you home before the snow starts." We walked over to his Range Rover and I got in, suddenly remembering the last time I'd ridden in it. A giggle escaped me and I covered my mouth with my hand.

"Something funny?" he asked, sliding behind the wheel and cocking his head.

"I might be a little punchy remembering the last time I was in your SUV."

He grinned as he put it in gear. "You mean you standing there in that hot-as-fuck pink wedding dress demanding I open the door like a lunatic?"

I dissolved into more giggles, nodding. "Yup."

Wait, had he just called me hot as fuck? Or was

he just talking about the dress? That was the same thing, right?

"It probably sucked when it was happening, but it's pretty funny now," he said as he turned out of the parking lot.

"I must've looked insane," I muttered. "Wedding dress, makeup running down my face…"

"It was more the serial killer look in your eyes than the makeup," he deadpanned.

I smiled, relaxing in the seat as I realized I'd already reached a point where I could laugh about that day. Probably not in front of my parents, but it felt easy with Boone.

Comfortable.

"Do you need a ride to work in the morning?" he asked as he pulled up to my building.

"I'm not sure," I admitted. "I have to figure out the car situation first. But I appreciate the offer."

"Anytime." He smiled over at me, the warmth in his eyes making my insides flutter.

"Would you like to come up for a drink?" I asked impulsively.

His eyes widened for a moment and he stared at me.

Crap.

I shouldn't have done that.

There was no doubt he was uncomfortable.

"I can't tonight," he said finally, looking away. "Early practice and all. Maybe another time."

"Oh, of course. Anyway, thanks for the ride. Good night."

I couldn't get out of that damn Range Rover fast enough.

What the hell had I been thinking?

CHAPTER NINE

Boone

I WAS SO FUCKING CLOSE. Those few seconds when I still had control were ticking by in a heartbeat. Though I knew I couldn't come yet, the urge was like a freight train barreling toward me—overpowering and unstoppable.

The woman riding my dick like her life depended on it threw her head back and cried out, her bright red hair flying through the air as she arched her back and sank down on me one last time. Now I could follow, and one thing was for fucking sure—the train was probably going to derail from the force of it.

A ringing sound roused me from the best dream

I'd had in a long time. I groaned and shoved away the pillow that was covering half of my face. When I grabbed my phone to turn off the alarm, there was no *Stop* button.

"The fuck?" I muttered, the ringing sound still going strong and my erection tenting the bedsheet.

Finally, it registered. It wasn't my phone's alarm; it was my doorbell. My downtown twelfth-floor condo had a doorbell that sounded like a gong through every inch of the apartment. And whoever was ringing it every two seconds seemed determined to wake me up from my epic dream.

I got up and pulled on the jeans I'd left on the floor, preparing myself to fight whoever was on the other side of the door. It was probably Lars, wanting to work out and go get breakfast on our only morning off in a while. We'd just returned from a long road trip, and I'd stayed up late last night playing video games because I wanted to sleep in today.

Just in case it was one of my neighbors, I put on a T-shirt right before heading out of my bedroom. The doorbell kept ringing.

Every. Two. Seconds. Someone had a death wish.

"Fuck, I'm coming," I grumbled.

I unlocked my door and opened it, not finding anyone there to scowl at.

"Hi," a small voice said.

I looked down and there was a little boy staring up at me, a stuffed elephant clutched under his arm.

"Oh, thank god," a female voice said.

When I focused on the speaker, who was getting up from her position sitting on the floor against the hallway wall, my jaw dropped.

It was my sister, Emma. Her hair was lighter and her face was thinner, and even though I was pissed at her for being out of contact with the family for so long, I was also relieved to see she was okay.

"Can we come in?" she asked.

"Uh…" I shook myself from the daze I was in. "Yeah, come in."

The boy walked inside, but I stepped in front of Emma before she could enter.

"Who is that?" I whispered. "Is that your kid?"

"Yeah, he's my son, Joey."

I narrowed my eyes at her. "How the fuck do you not tell your family you have a kid, Em? Do you have any idea how devastated Mom"

"Mikey, don't." Her hazel eyes swam with emotion. "I can't do this right now. I need help."

I assumed the help she needed could come by cash or check. And now that I knew she had a kid to support, everything had changed. I couldn't tell her to come back when she had her shit together.

"Okay." I stepped aside. "Come in."

Her face was etched with guilt and fatigue. Emma liked to say she had wanderlust, but what she really had was an inability to stick. When a job got stressful, or a relationship got tough, she moved on. My parents had tried to send her to college, but during first semester, Emma took off with a guy to travel the country in his van.

I didn't have to know anything about Joey to know he probably hadn't had an easy life.

"Joey, this is your Uncle Mikey," Emma said to him, getting down on her knees to help him take off his lined hoodie. "Should we see if he has snacks?"

"Can I have breakfast?" he asked.

It was after ten in the morning and the poor kid hadn't had breakfast. I swallowed my frustration for his sake.

"I can make you some bacon and eggs," I said. "Or pancakes."

"All of it," he said, his eyes brightening.

"You got it."

Emma led her son to the couch in my living room.

"Baby, Uncle Mikey and I are going to make breakfast while you watch a show, okay?"

He nodded. Emma grabbed my remote and looked up at me.

"How do you work this thing?"

"You want to watch a show or play a video game?" I asked Joey. "I have *Mario Brothers*."

"He's only four. He doesn't play video games," Emma said.

"Mario," Joey said.

I turned on the game and passed him a controller. His face lit up as he settled into the back of the couch and pushed buttons.

Emma followed me into the kitchen, where I started a pot of coffee before saying anything.

"I'm sorry to just drop in on you like this," she said.

I opened the fridge and got out bacon, eggs, butter, and milk, possible responses flying through my mind. Much as I wanted to, I couldn't dismiss my anger. She'd hurt our entire family.

"You know what's going on with Andy?" I asked her as I sat the food on the kitchen island.

She nodded. "It's one of the reasons I'm here. Do you know how he is?"

"The chemo's kicking his ass. We won't know if it's working until they finish this round of treatment and run some tests."

Emma smiled slightly. "I can't believe Andy's married with a kid. What's his wife like?"

I took out a big skillet and opened the package of

bacon. "Before you ask any questions, you need to answer some. Like where you've been for the past five years."

She furrowed her brow. "New Orleans, then a couple places in New Mexico. Joey's dad took off in Albuquerque and it's just been me and him since then."

"When was that?"

She shrugged. "Three years ago, I guess."

"How have you been supporting yourself?"

"By working," she said defensively.

"Yeah, but…how? With a kid to take care of?"

The coffee had brewed, so I poured two mugs and passed her one. She took a sip before continuing.

"He went to day care. We didn't have a lot, but I was doing okay."

I tensed as I placed slices of bacon in the skillet. "Was?"

She walked over to me, keeping her voice low. "Look, Mikey, I know what you think of me, but I'm a good mom. I love my son." Her voice wavered with emotion.

"I never said otherwise, Em."

"Yeah, but you asked me how I managed to take care of him, and I'm not some deadbeat who leaves my kid with other people so I can party. It's me and him, and that's it."

Tears pooled in her eyes, and I remembered what my dad always said before he died. *Family is all that really matters.* If he were here now, he'd want me to help Emma.

"I'm sorry," I said, meaning it. "I'm really glad you're here."

She blinked and tears slid down her cheeks. "I need your help."

I put a hand on her shoulder. "Listen, whatever it is, we'll get through it. If you owe people money, I'll pay them back. You don't need to bust your ass just to live anymore, okay?"

Emma looked like she was on the verge of tears again. "I'm sorry. There were so many times I wanted to call you, but I was too ashamed."

"Ashamed of what?"

She looked away. "All the times I asked Mom and Dad for money. Not showing up for Dad's funeral. I've been a terrible daughter and sister."

I knew she'd hit up our parents for $300 here and $500 there, and Andy and I had worried they were supporting a drug habit or a deadbeat boyfriend.

"What was the money for?" I asked her. "Be honest with me. I'm not going to judge you."

She sighed heavily. "Joey. Baby formula and diapers are really expensive, and for a while I didn't have residency anywhere and I couldn't get assistance. He's such a good kid, Mikey. He's my whole world, I swear it. I just want to be a good mom to him."

Relief coursed through me. I knew my sister, and I knew she was telling me the truth.

"I can feel how much you're dreading asking me for the help you need," I said. "Just tell me what it is."

She reached for a section of hair and toyed with the ends of it—an old nervous habit.

"I'm scared to even say it," she said, her voice barely audible.

"It's okay," I assured her. "I promise."

She met my eyes. "I've been drinking too much."

"Okay, keep talking."

I got a bowl and cracked a dozen eggs into it as she spoke.

"I only drink after Joey's in bed for the night. At first it was one glass a night, and if I was out of wine, I just didn't have one. But then it became two or three glasses, and I never let myself run out. I can't really afford the amount of wine I drink, but…" She looked at the ground. "I feel like I need it. I drink more than a bottle a night, and I can't make myself stop after a couple of glasses. If Joey would wake up and need me…"

This was tormenting her; I could hear it in her tone. As heartbreaking as it was to hear she was an alcoholic, at least she was ready to do something about it.

"I want to get better," she said. "For Joey."

"And for yourself," I added. "You deserve to be happy, Em. To not be weighed down by all this anymore. Is there a reason you drink?"

She shook her head. "It started out as a way to relax at the end of the day. Cleaning houses and waiting tables is hard work. I just wanted to unwind. But then…"

"I get it. Grandpa Boone was an alcoholic."

She met my eyes, both of us remembering the grandpa we never saw without a beer in hand. He never wanted to change, though, and his addiction eventually killed him.

"I found a twelve-week program I can get a scholarship for," she said. "It kills me to think of being away from Joey for that long, but I need to do it. I have to. Mikey, I need you to take care of Joey while I'm there. I don't want to ask Mom when Andy's so sick. It's too much."

I had no experience taking care of kids. It would completely upend my life. I'd have to hire help. But I didn't even have to think about it before I answered.

"Of course I'll take care of him."

Emma's eyes filled with tears again. "You will?"

I nodded. "You don't need to worry about him, just focus on what you need to do."

"Thank you, Mikey. There's no one else I trust with him, and…you were my only hope. The program's back in New Mexico, so I'll need to"

"Let's look into places here," I said. "Then maybe I could bring Joey to visit if they allow it. I'll pay for it."

She covered her face with her hands, quietly sobbing. I set down the whisk I'd just used on the eggs and pulled her into my arms.

"We're gonna get through this," I said. "You don't have to do this alone anymore, okay?"

"Thank you, Mikey," she said softly. "I love you."

"I love you, too."

After a minute or so, she pulled away and wiped her face. "I need to get it together so Joey doesn't see me like this. What can I do to help with breakfast?"

"Want to make pancakes?"

She grinned. "You know how amazing my pancakes are. Do you have any cinnamon?"

"If I do, it would be in the cabinet to the left of the stove."

I walked into the living room, where Joey was pushing buttons on the video game controller but not really accomplishing anything. He was a cute kid, his dark hair and hazel eyes reminding me of Andy at his age.

"Joey, you ready for some bacon and eggs?" I asked him. "And I'm about to start some toast."

He set the controller down and got up from the couch, stopping halfway to the kitchen to go back to the couch and get his stuffed elephant.

"I like your elephant, man," I said. "What's his name?"

"Trunkie."

I ruffled his hair. "We better get him some breakfast, too."

It had taken less than half an hour for my life to be turned completely upside down. I didn't want to tell Mom or Andy about Joey right now; they had enough on their plates. For now, I'd have to rely on my Mavericks family for help.

CHAPTER TEN

Jolie

I LEFT the lab early to go to the rink. I needed my skates sharpened and wanted to have a little time to decompress. Ellen had been on my case more than ever lately, and I couldn't figure out what it was. Jealousy? It didn't seem possible since she already had her PhD and I was still working on mine. She had a fiancé, and I'd only seen the guy from a distance a handful of times, so that couldn't have anything to do with it. It was just exhausting to be on my best behavior all the fucking time, like some kind of kid.

Academia came with its own set of pressures,

prejudices, and struggles, but it was the world I knew best. I was willing to work hard to get where I needed to be, even when that included kissing asses I didn't like and burning the candle at both ends to get everything done. But Ellen's personal attacks and ongoing torment seemed unfair.

Nothing in life is fair, I reminded myself as I handed my skates to Gil, the guy who ran the pro shop.

"Hey, Jolie." He smiled. "Give me about fifteen minutes, okay?"

"No rush. Thanks, Gil." I turned in time to see Boone coming into the rink with a little boy I'd never seen before.

I'd been planning to keep my distance from Boone after our embarrassing moment in the car, but my heart still skipped a beat when I saw him. That long, lean body. Broad shoulders with tapered hips. Those damn blue eyes. Why was it so hard to keep my emotions in check when he was around? Now he was heading toward me and even though I'd planned to find something else to do, I was curious about the little boy clinging to his hand while chattering animatedly.

Boone caught my eye and smiled, so I had no choice but to nod in acknowledgment, but before I could decide how to handle things, the little boy came running up to me.

"Are you a mermaid?" he demanded breathlessly. He had the same blue eyes as Boone and I was momentarily stunned. Did Boone have a son I'd never heard about?

Oh shit, was he involved with someone?

My intention the other night had been clear, so if he had a girlfriend somewhere, I'd be even more embarrassed.

"You're Ariel, right?" the little boy continued.

I squatted down so we were eye level. "Nope. My name is Jolie."

His face turned down in a frown. "But you're Ariel," he insisted. He reached out and gently pulled a lock of my hair. "Like from *The Little Mermaid.*"

"Joey." Boone's voice was firm but gentle. "You can't pull a girl's hair."

"I didn't pull it," he insisted, turning to him. "I just wanted to touch it. But she said she's not Ariel."

"That's right." Boone scooped him up, grinning. "This is my friend Jolie. She's another coach here at hockey camp."

"You're not a mermaid?" Joey turned to me almost accusingly and I laughed.

"I'm sorry, no. I wish I was a mermaid, but no

tail, see?" I held out my right foot and wiggled it a little.

Joey laughed.

"This is my nephew, Joey," Boone said. "My sister's son. He'll be staying with me for a while." The look he gave me told me there was a lot more to the story but that we shouldn't talk about it in front of Joey.

I nodded, a relief I couldn't explain surging through me.

It wasn't his kid.

Not that his having a child would have changed anything on my part, but at least this meant I hadn't hit on someone in a relationship.

"Do you play hockey?" I asked Joey.

He shook his head sadly. "No. But Mommy says Uncle Mikey can teach me!"

"What did I tell you to call me, buddy?"

Joey grinned up at him. "Uncle Boone! Like your hockey buddies!"

"Right." Boone ruffled his hair. "Hang on while I go find you some skates, okay?"

"Okay." Joey seemed happy to sit on the nearest bench, playing with a stuffed elephant that looked well loved.

"Walk with me, Jolie?" he asked.

"Uh, sure." I fell into step next to him.

"I wanted to apologize for the other night," he said softly.

"Oh, it's okay." This was the last thing I wanted to talk about.

"No, it's not." He stopped and turned to me. "I didn't mean to seem like I was blowing you off. That wasn't it at all. I wanted to come upstairs, but I'm worried—"

"Uncle Boone, look!" Joey came racing over to us, pointing at the ice. "Is that the zologna?" He pronounced it like bologna but with a *Z*.

"It's called a Zamboni," Boone said, cracking up.

I laughed too.

"Can I ride it?" Joey asked, his eyes wide with excitement.

"Not today," Boone said. "But I'll ask and maybe next time, okay?"

Joey's face fell.

"We'll make it happen," I whispered to him. "But there isn't enough time today, okay?"

"Thanks, Jolie." His little grin melted my heart.

He ran to the glass to watch the ice being cleaned and Boone followed him with his eyes. "Poor kid. Emma's a great mom, but she's been through a lot."

"How long will he be staying with you?" I asked politely, unsure how to get back to the conversation we'd been having before so he could explain what he was worried about.

Boone sighed. "I don't know. Emma—" He stopped abruptly and looked around, dropping his voice as if he didn't want anyone to hear us. "She just went into rehab. It's looking like twelve weeks."

"What about his dad?"

He shook his head. "Gone. Left them."

"Dickhead."

"Tell me about it."

"What will you do when you travel?" I asked. It was none of my business, but I couldn't help myself.

"Wes's wife Hadley has said she'll keep him sometimes and Sheridan the rest of the time. Just depends on who's feeling the best since both of them are pregnant."

"I can help," I said, the words tumbling out before I could stop them. "I'm done with the research part of my dissertation, so now I just have to write the thing, and I can do that from anywhere most of the time. And maybe when you're traveling, if he enjoys coming, I can pick him up and bring him here with me for a couple of hours to give Hadley or Sheridan a break."

"You'd do that for me?" His eyes met mine and something lurked behind them I couldn't quite decipher. These were the times I got the feeling he was into me, despite his rejection the other night.

"Hey, like Dad always says, the Mavericks are a family, and this is important. I don't mind at all. We can talk before the next road trip and figure out a schedule for whatever you need."

"Thanks, Jolie." He nodded solemnly. "I mean it."

"Of course." I glanced toward the pro shop, where Gil was waving at me. "I guess my skates are ready, but I'll see you on the ice."

"For sure. And we're going to finish our conversation," he called after me.

We were?

Oh boy.

I didn't know what that meant, but I liked the sound of it.

———

As usual, I was late the next morning. We didn't have nine-to-five hours since we often worked until late in the night, and that was what I had planned for tonight. Hockey camp was closed for two days for ice refurbishing, so I would be here at the lab as long as I could keep my eyes open.

"Good morning!" Corrine called out in her usual

cheerful voice. Today, however, she handed me a cup from Starbucks.

"What's this?" I asked curiously.

Her eyes met mine with a silent message that told me something was going on.

"Coffee for all my favorite scientists," she said in a tone that didn't match the look on her face. "Grande white chocolate mocha, right? With whipped cream."

"Good for my taste buds, less so for my figure," I murmured, taking a sip and watching her over the rim of the cup.

"I just thought we could all use a little treat, so I ran out."

"Uh-huh." I gazed over at Dr. Matello's office, where he and Ellen seemed to be deep in conversation. "What's that about?"

"No idea, but I figured we could at least be armed with caffeine. Just in case. They've been in there since seven thirty this morning."

"I don't even need to be here today," I murmured.

Whatever was going on in there probably didn't have anything to do with me, but even if it did, I couldn't control it. All I could control was what I was doing, which was the data I was helping Ellen gather and writing my dissertation.

I would have loved to tell Ellen to fuck off, but

that would be a betrayal of my PI. Dr. Matello was counting on me to help Ellen with her analysis so she could move ahead to the next phase of her work, but my original thought was that I'd be done with all that once I got married. Since that hadn't happened, I'd somehow gotten sucked back in and it was becoming problematic. I was in the process of trying to get grant money for what I was going to work on next because I couldn't rely on my parents financially forever. I didn't have a postdoctoral job lined up yet, so that had to be my next priority.

On top of that, I'd really begun to enjoy coaching at the rink. I loved science, and that was going to be my future, but it didn't mean I had to be one-dimensional. I could also love hockey and donate my time coaching kids who didn't have the opportunities I'd had. It felt like the right thing to do at this stage of my life.

MY PHONE RANG and I was surprised to see Hadley Kirby's name on the screen. She was married to the Mavericks' team captain, Wes, and I'd met her a handful of times but didn't know her that well.

"Hello?"

"Jolie? Hi, this is Hadley Kirby."

"Hi, Hadley."

"Do you have a minute to talk?"

"Sure."

"I was talking with Boone and he said you'd volunteered to help out with Joey on the team's next road trip. I thought it might be both fun and useful for everyone if we got together to come up with a schedule. That way, us ladies who are going to be doing most of the work will have a chance to get organized, the kids can have a playdate, and we can hang out."

"That sounds great," I said. "I'm still in grad school, so I spend a lot of time at my lab, but I can be flexible if you give me warning."

"I was thinking Saturday around eleven. The guys leave Friday, so Joey will already be here."

"I'll be there," I said warmly. "Thanks for reaching out."

"Thanks for volunteering to help."

"Of course. Anything I can do."

"Then I'll see you Saturday."

"I'm looking forward to it."

I disconnected and took another sip of the coffee. If I was really quick, maybe I could toss my coat on the back of my chair, lock up my purse, and escape to the library with my laptop. I could hide deep in the stacks surrounded by aged and yellowed bound journals, maybe find a dusty, shadowy corner and work in peace. Ellen would never think to look for me there and if I made some headway, I'd be able to focus on Joey over the weekend instead of writing. Feeling better about the rest of the week, I took a quick look around, grabbed my laptop, and slipped out the door.

CHAPTER ELEVEN

Boone

JOEY USED both hands to pick up the giant slice of cheese pizza on his plate, biting off the end before setting it down and giving me a serious look.

"When will my mom be back?"

"Not for a while, bud. She's working on something important. Remember when we talked about it before she had to leave?"

He looked down at his plate. "I want her to come back."

Damn. In the past couple of days, I'd discovered that being a full-time uncle was tough. Joey was a good kid who didn't ask for much, but I had to feed or entertain him every waking minute of the day. An intern from the front office had hung out with him at the arena while I was at practice, and Hadley had put herself in charge of scheduling his care when I was traveling. I was grateful for the help but still overwhelmed by my new responsibility.

"I know she misses you," I said. "But what she's doing is really important, so we have to support her."

"What does that mean?"

His dark hair hung down to the tips of his long eyelashes, and I reminded myself again to take him to my barber for a haircut as soon as possible.

"It means you and me have to help each other out while she's away. Like how you helped me with the dishes earlier."

I figured the busier he was, the less he'd miss Emma, so I'd asked him to unload the dishwasher and fold towels earlier. The towels were already folded, but I unfolded every single one I could find in the linen closet and we'd refolded them together. He'd learned to fold towels and put away dishes; I'd learned that everything takes three times longer when you're doing it with a kid's help.

"I want some orange soda," he said.

Upside. When he talked about missing Emma, he never lingered on it for long, which was good.

Downside. I was pretty sure my sister never gave the kid anything but orange soda to drink, which we were going to have a talk about later.

"We don't have soda here in St. Louis," I said. "Just water and milk."

"No soda?"

"Nope."

He believed anything I told him, which made my life easier. I walked over to the fridge and got him a bottle of water, opening it and setting it in front of him.

"So how did you like hockey camp?" I asked him.

He shrugged. "I fell down a lot."

"Everyone falls at first. You just keep getting back up and you'll get the hang of it."

When I saw him in skates and hockey gear at camp last night, I'd felt a surge of pride. My nephew was going to be a hockey player. I had twelve weeks to make him fall in love with it.

"You'll have kids to play with at Wes and Hadley's," I said. "And lots of toys."

Joey's face lit up with happiness. "What kind of toys?"

"All kinds. They have a whole room of toys. They even have a big treehouse thing in the basement you can climb on."

"Do they have any robots?"

"I'm not sure, but I bet they do. You won't get bored over there."

He gave me a solemn look. "When are you coming back?"

Poor kid. His mom was the only caregiver he'd ever known. She'd left him, and though it was for a good reason, he was too young to understand it. Now I was leaving him when he'd only been with me for a couple of days. I had to, though. I couldn't miss games unless I had a life-or-death emergency.

"I'm leaving in the morning and taking you over to Wes and Hadley's house right before I go," I said. "I'll be gone for three nights. We can FaceTime while I'm gone."

"What's that?"

"You'll see. It's pretty cool."

He nodded and said, "Okay."

"Do you have an iPad?" I asked him.

"No."

He'd arrived with just a backpack filled with a few changes of clothes and his stuffed elephant. Emma said she'd been hanging on by a thread, their few possessions in the car she'd stored at my place. I knew I shouldn't buy him all the things she wasn't able to, but I wanted to spoil him just a little bit.

"I'll get you one and have someone bring it to Wes and Hadley's," I said. "That way we can FaceTime."

"Can I see my mom?"

"Hopefully soon," I said. "You want any more pizza?"

He shook his head.

"Okay, let's clean up and then we're going to do something fun."

"What?"

I picked up his paper plate, stacked it on mine and then tossed them both in the trash.

"Have you ever been to a trampoline park?" I asked him.

"I've been to a park. It had a really big slide."

"I think you'll like this place. We get to bounce on trampolines. You'll either get to see me do a backflip or kick myself in the face trying to do one."

Joey laughed.

"Which one would you rather see?" I asked him, grinning. "The backflip or me kicking myself in the face."

"Kicking yourself in the face," he said, laughing harder.

I'd put a smile on his face, and that was a win. If it made him laugh like that, I'd kick myself anytime.

"WHAT'S WITH THE LIMP?" Nash said to me in a low tone the next morning as I sat down next to him on the bus that was taking the team to the airport for our road trip.

"It's nothing," I whispered. "Drop it."

"It's not nothing if I noticed it. Did you hurt your ankle or something?"

I glared at him. "Are you capable of shutting the fuck up? Have you ever, just once in your life, closed your giant face hole for five full minutes?"

"My giant face hole? There's a porn title in there somewhere."

I rolled my eyes, tired from a long night of Joey waking me up multiple times to tell me he couldn't sleep.

"I saw a good one the other day," he said, smirking. "*Smoking Cracks.*"

"You saw the title or actually watched the movie?"

He shrugged. "It was no *Sperminator*. Didn't merit a full viewing."

Nash collected funny porno titles like other people collected stamps. *Pulp Friction. Throbin Hood. Sorest Rump.* We'd heard them all, more than once.

"Seriously, what's up with the ankle?" he said.

"It's fine. I tweaked it at the trampoline park last night, but once it's taped, it won't be a problem."

He looked confused, but then awareness dawned on his face. "You took Joey there."

"Yep."

"And?"

And I'd achieved Rock Star Uncle status.

"He fucking loved it. We closed the place down. It took me about fifty tries, but I can still do a backflip."

Nash looked over the top of the seat in front of us and then behind us. "Dude, don't say that here. If Coach finds out, your ass will be in a sling."

I nodded because he was right. We were paid too much to be doing backflips on trampolines during the season. The risk of injury was too high. I sure as hell wasn't going to tell the trainers why I needed my ankle taped.

This job was a dream, but it wasn't always the walk in the park people on the outside thought it was. We weren't allowed to have off days. We couldn't go rock climbing or parasailing like normal people. Every player on the team was seen as an investment; we could have the shit beaten out of us every night on the ice, but off of it, we had to be careful. The irony.

"Hey," Wes said as he walked past us. "Joey was

doing good when I left. He was playing Candyland with Annalise."

I turned so I could see him as he settled into the unoccupied seat behind us. "Good."

Wes shrugged. "Good for Annalise. She cheats at Candyland like you wouldn't believe."

"I'm sure Joey's just glad to have another kid to play with."

"Hadley sent our housekeeper to pick up orange soda for him," Wes said. "Anything else he really likes?"

I shook my head. "Tell her not to get him all sugared up."

"That's all we feed our kids," Wes said in a level tone. "It's just bowls of sugar for every meal."

"I want Joey to still have teeth when he hits puberty," I said.

Wes grinned. "I hear you, boss. But the kid's been through a lot in the past few days. We figured if some orange soda would make him happy, we'll get him some orange soda."

He was right. Why hadn't I thought about it that way?

"I owe you guys," I said. "Well, just Hadley, really. You aren't doing shit. Tell her I'll take the kids so she can go to a spa for the weekend sometime."

"Shit," Wes said, laughing. "You wouldn't survive

it. Benny rides down the stairs naked in a laundry basket. Kid's a daredevil. He was sliding down the banister in the buff, but the chafing wised him up real quick."

"And you guys are having another one," Nash said, cringing. "You'd better get snipped after this one."

"Nah, we want more," Wes said. "It's chaos, but it's our chaos."

Wes and Hadley getting custody of our former team captain Ben and Lauren's kids when they passed away had changed him. He was more laid back now, more self-assured, and happier than I'd ever seen him. He'd given Hadley a diamond pendant necklace, in the shape of a star, for Christmas and told her it was because she was his North Star, always helping him find his direction.

I wanted what they had. Not all the kids—at least, not yet—but an all-in love that erased all doubts. Wes called Hadley from the road all the time because she was the person that he wanted to talk to. He never made big decisions without talking to her first. They were a team, and they were crazy about each other. I'd thought I found the one last year, but when I proposed, she shot me down.

"Let's get this show on the road, boys," Wes said,

putting on his noise-canceling headphones as he settled into his seat.

I did the same, so I wouldn't have to listen to Nash yapping about porn titles the whole way to the airport. Within five minutes, I felt myself falling asleep.

CHAPTER TWELVE

Jolie

"Well, who's this?" Grandma G smiled at Joey as I helped her into the passenger seat of my Jeep.

"Grandma, this is Joey. Joey, this is my grandmother, Mrs. Gizzard."

Grandma gave me a look before turning to Joey. "You can just call me Grandma," she told him.

"Hi, Grandma!" He grinned, waving at her with his elephant.

"Lunch is probably going to be a little louder than you're used to," I said, getting behind the wheel. "But I wanted to find a place where he could run around a little while we talk and eat."

"They have a lot of energy at that age," she said, smiling.

"They do." Boy, was that an understatement. I'd taken him to hockey camp last night, which had been fine, but then Hadley had called early this morning saying Benny had a fever and she was worried that whatever he had might be contagious. I'd blown off going to the lab and had picked Joey up instead. We'd run a few errands and then I'd called Grandma G to see if she felt like going to lunch.

Now we were on our way.

There was a buffet-style all-you-can-eat pizza place that had a small game room in the back, so I figured Joey could eat and then I'd give him a few bucks to play games while Grandma and I caught up.

"I love pizza!" Joey announced, his mouth full.

"Me too," Grandma G agreed, though her plate was full of salad at the moment.

"That's salad," Joey pointed out needlessly.

"Salad first, then pizza for me," she said.

"Yuck." He took another bite of pizza and then stood up. "Can I go play now?"

I wanted to tell him to finish eating first, but what difference did it make? He'd come back when he was hungry. The play area was gated, with no exits, so I could relax and finish my own lunch.

"Go on," I said gently, pulling a few dollars out of my purse. "Do you know how to buy tokens?"

"From the machine!" He nodded, snatching the money out of my hand before taking off.

"He's a ball of energy," Grandma G said.

"He's a good kid. I don't mind helping out."

She eyed me. "Tell me about you and Boone."

"Oh." I was pretty sure my cheeks got red, but I tried to play it off. "There's nothing to tell. We're just friends. You know, from hockey camp."

She laughed. "I was born in the morning, sweetheart. But not this morning. Every time his name comes up, your eyes sparkle."

"They do not," I muttered.

"It's okay to like him," she said. "Why are you acting weird?"

"Because even if he was interested, and I'm not sure he is, Dad would never allow it. So what's the point?"

"Your father is a good man, but he's not God. He can't determine who you should be with, no matter how hard he wants to try. He chose Jarvis for you and we all know how that turned out."

"Yeah, but Boone has to think about his career and Dad basically controls it."

"So you do like him."

"What's not to like? Gorgeous, successful,

athletic, rich, a good brother and uncle from what I've seen. He ticks off a lot of boxes. But the truth is we barely know each other."

"And yet here you are, taking care of little Joey. Seems to me there's something there, whether you want to acknowledge it or not."

"Maybe." I chewed my lip thoughtfully. "There's something about him. I can't explain it."

"I knew I was going to marry your grandfather the first time I saw him. Sometimes all it takes is a split second and your soul understands before the rest of you gets on board."

"I had no idea you were such a romantic," I said, smiling at her.

"I wasn't always old, you know. And even though my body is falling apart, on the inside, I'm still a woman with wants and needs and memories. It manifests itself differently now, of course, but it never goes away. So don't waste time, my love." She put one of her hands over mine. "I don't know if Boone is the right man for you or if there's anything there, but don't be afraid to find out. Life passes you by in the blink of an eye."

"You must miss Grandpa a lot."

"More than you know." She daintily dabbed her napkin across her mouth. "Now, there's some kind of cheeseburger pizza that's calling my name. Excuse me while I indulge."

"I'll be here." I watched her go with a fond smile before turning to see what Joey was doing.

He was standing on a small step stool playing pinball and he was so intense I couldn't resist taking a few pictures to send to Boone.

To my surprise, he responded almost immediately.

BOONE: *Someone looks like they're getting spoiled.*

JOLIE: *No idea what you're talking about. LOL*

BOONE: *Is he behaving?*

JOLIE: *He's very well-behaved. We're having lunch with my grandmother. Well, he already ate and now he's becoming a pinball wizard while we finish eating.*

BOONE: *Excellent. Hadley texted to say Benny has strep and Joey is staying with you until I get home. Are you sure that's okay?*

JOLIE: *Better me than Sheridan. I can afford to get strep if he has it, but she can't. It's no problem at all.*

BOONE: *Our flight gets in around nine. Is it all right if I come by to pick him up that late?*

JOLIE: *Of course. I'll be up working on my dissertation.*

BOONE: *Then I'll see you then.*

JOLIE: *See you tonight.*

I looked up from my phone and smiled.

———

I'D PUT Joey to sleep on my bed so he wouldn't be disturbed by me typing away on my laptop, and I was buried in all things microbiology when a soft knock on the door made me jump.

Boone.

I got up quickly and fluffed my hair, wiping my hands on my jeans.

Why was I nervous?

He was just here to pick up Joey.

It wasn't like anything was going on between us.

But my grandmother's words had resonated with me and I realized that I'd been hiding behind science and my education for so long, at some point I'd stopped living. Even when I'd been with Jarvis, my mind had always been on my studies, my PhD, things like that. Since the breakup, I'd added hockey to my arsenal of ways to distract myself from life in general, but deep down I recognized that something was missing.

I hadn't been able to articulate it until today, but Boone made me want to feel again. It made no sense, but it seemed like I should try to find out why. We'd never finished our conversation from that night at the rink, and I wanted to.

"Hi." I opened the door and motioned him inside.

"Hey." He looked road weary and slightly tousled but deliciously hot in the suit he'd obviously been traveling in. His broad shoulders seemed to fill the small room as he stood there looking around.

"Joey asleep?" he asked.

"Yeah. I put him in my bed so I could potentially watch TV or something, but I've been working."

"I really appreciate you stepping up like this."

"It's not a problem." I cocked my head. "You look wiped. Are you hungry? I could make you a sandwich. Nothing fancy, but I have turkey and Swiss, a ciabatta roll…"

He met my gaze hesitantly. "I could eat. You sure you don't mind? It's late and you've had Joey all day."

"Don't be ridiculous. It's just a sandwich. Come on." I led him into my tiny kitchen and he perched on one of the two barstools that made up what I called the dining room, even though it was nothing but an extended counter that overlooked the main room. I got out lunch meat, cheese, mayonnaise, and mustard and put everything in front of him before slicing a roll in half and putting it on a plate.

"Something to drink? I think I have water and one bottle of Corona, but you're welcome to it."

He chuckled. "Water's good. Thanks."

I got him a bottle of water while he made his sandwich and then we were quiet for a few minutes.

"This really hit the spot," he said, wiping his mouth with a napkin and downing the rest of his water. "I slept on the plane and didn't get dinner. I was hungrier than I thought."

"Glad I could help." I put the dish and knife he'd used in the sink, surprised to find him behind me as I turned.

"Hey."

Holy shit, he was really close.

Close enough to catch the faint scent of a woodsy aftershave.

"I want to explain what happened when I dropped you off that night," he said quietly, his eyes fixed on mine.

"I understand," I whispered.

"No, you don't." He lifted a hand, gently brushing my hair back from my face. "I like you. You're smart and beautiful and really brave. Walking out on your wedding that day took guts, which is something I respect."

"I suspect there's a *but* coming," I murmured, unable to tear my gaze away from his.

"Your father," he said quietly. "He's been crystal clear that his daughter is off-limits, and I'm not sure that's a line I can cross."

"I'm an adult," I said. "A grown, independent woman who can make her own choices and decisions about who she spends her time with. Dad is going to have to get over this need to choose a husband for me. I can't live my life like that and I don't think you should let him control you either. There's no reason we can't be friends. Or whatever."

"Or whatever?" A faint smile played on his lips as he continued to look down at me. "What kind of whatever are we talking about?"

"This kind." With my grandmother's words zinging through my subconscious and giving me courage, I leaned up and lightly pressed my lips to his.

"Mmm. I like your idea of whatever." He slid his hands around my waist, drawing me closer. His fingers were gentle, holding me in place as he slanted his head over mine. Our lips parted this time, coming together with a sensual mixture of caution and curiosity.

I'd never made the first move like that before, but it felt right with Boone.

Kissing him was unlike anything I'd ever experienced. He was in no rush, brushing his lips across mine, across my cheek, under my chin, as if he could stand here and kiss me all night. And yet, there was an underlying urgency that left no doubt about his desire for me.

"Fuck, you taste sweet." He put his hands on

either side of my face. "I never want to stop kissing you, gorgeous…"

"I don't want you to."

"I'd like to take you out on a date," he whispered, one hand palming my ass as the other dug into the hair at the base of my skull. "Dinner…" He trailed his tongue along my jaw, making goose bumps break out on my skin. "Maybe dancing…" His breath was warm against my cheek. "A nightcap at my place."

"Mmm." Words eluded me. He was barely touching me, yet my body tingled with arousal.

"Then—" He cut off abruptly as a cry came from the bedroom.

"Joey!" We moved in unison, rushing to my room and throwing open the door.

The boy was thrashing around on the bed, obviously having a nightmare, his little face screwed up in either pain or fear.

"Hey, buddy." I slid into bed next to him, wrapping my arms around his small body. "Hey, wake up. It's just a dream. Joey?"

His eyes snapped open and he jerked in surprise before recognition dawned and he relaxed against me.

"Look who's here," I whispered, stroking his hair.

"Uncle Boone!" He threw himself into Boone's

arms the moment he saw him, curling against his chest.

"What were you dreaming about, big guy?" Boone asked, cradling him.

"A monster." Joey's voice broke. "It was big and black with red teeth. It was chasing mommy and she was running and crying."

"It's just a dream. Mommy's working on something important, remember? But she's fine. And she'll be back before you know it."

"Promise?"

"I promise." Boone's eyes met mine across the bed and I nodded encouragement, thinking what a great dad he was going to be someday.

"I'll get his backpack," I whispered, sliding off the bed.

I'd already gathered Joey's things earlier in anticipation of Boone's late arrival, so I was surprised to feel his hand on my back a moment later.

"Date night," he said under his breath. "As soon as we can make it happen between practice, games, camp, your schedule, and Joey's."

"We'll figure it out."

He stroked his knuckles across my cheek. "You can count on it."

"Good night, Boone."

"Good night, gorgeous." He threw Joey's backpack over his shoulder and then scooped the boy up as he padded out of the bedroom.

"See you tomorrow," I called to Joey.

"Bye, Jolie." Joey's eyes were already closing as his head landed on Boone's shoulder.

"Soon," Boone mouthed to me.

I leaned against the door after I'd closed it behind them, taking a moment to let the evening's developments wash over me.

I'd kissed Boone.

Then he'd kissed me back.

And we were going out on a date.

"Thanks, Grandma," I whispered.

CHAPTER THIRTEEN

Boone

ANDY PICKED up the phone on the first ring, sounding more like himself than he had in a long time.

"Hey, Mikey, how are you?" he said.

"Can't complain. You busy?"

"Not really. Carrie's still at work and Mom took Mason to the grocery store. We're making lasagna when they get back."

Dishes clinked in the background. That meant he was out of bed, which was great.

"What are you doing while they're gone?" I asked.

"I'm emptying the dishwasher." He laughed. "I know it sounds stupid, but this is the stuff I miss the most when I'm down for a few days after treatment. I did three loads of laundry today and it was awesome."

If only he could see my house. I was lucky to get the dishes done once a day with Joey here. Caring for him had given me a newfound respect for anyone who took care of young kids.

"When's your next treatment?" I asked him.

"In a couple of weeks. I'm starting a cedar chest for Mom in my workshop, hoping to get it done before the next treatment. Don't tell her, though. It's a Mother's Day gift."

I scoffed and grinned at the same time. "You douchebag. That's an epic gift. Now I can't just send flowers without your gift making me look bad."

"I mean, you can. The favorite kid has to do something extra special for her, so you're off the hook."

"Favorite, my ass."

He cleared his throat. "Hey, while I'm by myself, I wanted to tell you…Emma called Mom."

My heart rate kicked up at the mention of our sister's name. Joey was over at Lars and Sheridan's house because they were hosting a sleepover for all the Mavericks' kids tonight. Their new house had an indoor pool, so the kids had all gone over midafternoon to swim.

"Really?" I said, not sure whether I wanted to let him know I'd heard from her, too.

"She said she's starting rehab. Mom said she sounded better than she has in a long time. She didn't ask Mom for anything, either. She just wanted to apologize and tell her she's working on getting better."

"Yeah, I actually heard from her, too. She came to my apartment and I'm the one who took her to rehab."

I could hear dishes being set down, then silence. "Seriously? Why didn't you say anything?"

"I thought about it, but…I knew you were feeling like shit from treatment, and…I had my reasons for not telling Mom."

After a beat, Andy said, "Dude, this is me. You can tell me. My body's sick, but my mind is the same as ever."

I immediately felt guilty for not saying anything sooner. My brother and I had always been close. He was the one I'd call if I was in a jam and vice versa.

"Okay, well…don't tell Mom because it's Emma's place to do it, but, uh…"

"Just say it, fuck. Is she sick? Please don't tell me she has cancer."

"She has a kid."

A few seconds of silence passed and Andy exhaled hard. "Wow. I didn't see that coming."

"Yeah, his name is Joey and he's four. And he's staying with me while she's at rehab."

Andy let out a full-throated laugh and I furrowed my brow, confused.

"What?" I said.

"You're serious?" he said, sobering. "You?"

What the fuck? Like it was so hard to imagine me taking care of my own nephew?

"Yes, me. My teammates' wives and my coach's daughter are helping me."

"What's he like? Has she taken care of him? Shit, that poor kid."

I immediately felt defensive on Emma's behalf. For all her faults, I knew she was a good mom. That was the whole reason she was enduring the shame of admitting her alcoholism and going to rehab.

"He's a great kid. He's at a sleepover at one of my teammates' houses tonight. I'll send you some pictures, but this stays between us, okay?"

"Yeah, of course."

I heard female voices in the background, and Andy said, "I'm talking to Mikey."

"Mikey!" my mom said. "Ask him why he never calls his mother anymore."

I smiled, wishing I was standing in Andy and

Carrie's kitchen with them. "Tell her I'll call her tomorrow and I wish I could eat her lasagna tonight. I have to go. I've got to get ready for a date."

"A date? Mikey has a date!"

Mom and Carrie squealed in the background.

"Don't wear a V-neck! No woman wants to see your chest hair coming out the top of your shirt!" Mom called. "And don't cheap out on dinner!"

Andy chuckled into the phone.

"Tell her I don't own any V-necks and we're going to Chick-fil-A," I said. "I'll catch you later, man."

"Bye."

Andy ended the call and I set my phone down, picked up the refrigerator magnets Joey had scattered on the floor and then headed for the shower. I was looking forward to having Jolie all to myself this evening for the first time since I'd helped her escape on her wedding day.

———

"AM I TOO DRESSED UP?" Jolie asked as our eyes met when she opened the front door of her apartment.

I liked her in her sweats and stocking caps, but tonight she was stunning in a simple black dress with a V-neck and long sleeves, her hair pulled up with a few loose pieces resting against her porcelain skin.

She'd dressed up for *me*. The woman who had been off-limits since the moment I'd seen her was telling me it was okay to look at her and it was okay to want her.

And fuck, did I want her. All I could think about was pushing that dress up to her hips, cupping her ass in my hands to pull her close, and devouring her mouth. I wanted to feel every inch of her.

"You look perfect," I said with a grin.

She looked down at the dress and then back up at me. "So I had shapewear on under the dress, but it was smashing my internal organs, so I just took it off and now I'm all sweaty."

I arched a brow, amused and delighted by her complete honesty. "And here I thought that glow was because of me."

"Maybe some of it is," she said, smiling.

"I think your shape is perfect as it is, and I'm sure we'll both have a better time if your internal organs aren't smashed, so…shall we?"

I held out an arm to her and she took it, putting the strap of her purse over her other shoulder.

"Hold that thought," she said. "I need your arm because I hardly ever wear heels, but I have to lock the door first."

I shamelessly ogled her as she turned around to lock the door. She was tall and curvy in all the right places, and her black heels were sexy as fuck. I didn't want them to hurt her feet, though.

"Hey, you sure you want to wear the heels?" I asked. "You can leave them with the shapewear and be comfortable if you want."

She shrugged. "I hardly ever get to dress up and feel pretty. I stuck a pair of flats in my bag in case I need to change later."

Our eyes locked and a slight flush crept over her cheeks. My heart pounded in my chest just from looking at her. What was happening here? I'd seen Jolie many times in the years I'd been playing hockey here, but I'd never seen her like this. She wasn't just my coach's daughter or my fellow volunteer youth hockey coach; she was also a strong, smart, sexy woman I couldn't get enough of.

I wanted to take her out on the town and show her a good time. I also wanted to curl up on the couch with her. Take her to bed. Talk about our lives until the sun rose. In this one moment, I wanted everything all at once.

"Ready?" she asked.

"I...yeah, sorry. I'm ready." I ran a hand through my hair. "I've really been looking forward to this."

"Me too. I'll try not to talk your ear off about

studying regulatory patterns of gene expression. I spent the day writing a report about the subject, so it's on my mind."

"I don't mind. I'd actually like to hear more about what you do."

"Really?"

She sounded so genuinely surprised that I knew Jarvis hadn't shown any interest in her studies. He'd never deserved her.

"I'll tell you more about it later," she said on the walk to the car. "First I want to hear about how breakfast turned out."

I laughed as she took my arm. "If you don't mind lots of shells in your scrambled eggs, it was fantastic."

Joey and I had made breakfast together this morning and ended up with doughy pancakes, crunchy eggs, and slightly burned toast.

"Aw, he looked so proud in that photo you sent me of him standing on a chair flipping a pancake."

"He had a good time. We're kind of getting a crash course in each other, you know? Since we hadn't met before this."

She smiled at me as we stopped next to my car. "You're doing an amazing job with him."

"I couldn't do it without you and Sheridan and Hadley."

I opened the door and she kept her hold on my arm as she got in.

"I love spending time with him," she said. "Did I tell you he asked my grandma where she got her wrinkles?"

I cringed. "Oh shit, he did?"

"My grandma loved it. She told him wrinkles are secret hiding places for magic. He was blown away."

"She sounds like a good sport."

"The best."

I couldn't bring myself to close the door. Instead, I leaned closer to her, my hands on the doorframe of my Range Rover. Her breath hitched as I gently leaned my forehead against hers, taking in the light, sweet scent of her perfume.

"Did I mention how amazing you look tonight?" I asked.

"Hmm, I don't think so," she said playfully.

I brushed my lips against hers. She kissed me back and put a hand around my neck, her fingers sliding into my hair.

"I've never seen anyone so beautiful," I murmured against her lips.

She inhaled and exhaled softly. "You don't have to say that."

"It's the truth. Seeing your hair up like that is making me crazy."

Her hum held promise. "Maybe you'll get to see it down later."

If I didn't move away from her, I'd never be able to. I was rock hard. It took all my strength to push back from the car, groaning with frustration as I shut the door.

When I got settled in the driver's side seat, I looked over at her, noting that her skin had that slight pink flush again. I wasn't sure how much more I could take.

"Just dinner," she said. "I know you said dinner and drinks and maybe a stop at Lars and Sheridan's, but I was thinking just dinner and then we can come back here."

"Fuck yes." I started the car, looking in the rearview mirror before pulling into traffic.

I was relieved we were on the same page, but something was nagging at me. It had been on my mind since my conversation with Andy.

"There's something I need to tell you," I said.

She looked over at me with a serious expression on her face. "Oh no, this doesn't sound good."

I sighed heavily. "I really like you, Jolie. A lot."

"Oh god. Just get to it already," she said.

"There's not really a *but*. It's just that I'm trying to get traded to Nashville, and I want to be up front with you about it."

"Nashville?"

"It's not about hockey. It's because of my family. I need to be closer to them right now."

She nodded, and I could tell she was thinking about what I'd said. I hoped like hell I hadn't just blown my chance with her.

"My brother"

She cut me off. "You don't have to tell me. As long as you're completely single, let's just have a good night together, okay? And if you're still here and we want to keep seeing each other after that, we will. I don't know where I'm going to end up, either, but probably not here. Let's just enjoy right now, okay?"

I smiled, relieved and more impressed by her than ever. "Yeah, that sounds perfect."

CHAPTER FOURTEEN

Jolie

I'D NEVER BEEN a person who played games with others. I understood there were rituals and expectations that went along with dating. Playing hard to get, not sleeping with someone on the first date—unless it was a one-night stand—and not scarfing down a massive steak. Those were things we learned as women, even studious, academic sorts like me. Yet all of that flew right out the window with Boone. He didn't make me feel like I had to pretend to be someone else, not like Jarvis always had. In fact, Boone made me feel like the real me was the absolute best version there could be. And no one else had ever made me feel that way.

When we sat down at a popular high-end steak house and he suggested the Tomahawk rib eye for two, which included lobster tails and sides that made my mouth water, I didn't hesitate to say yes. I didn't say no to wine or the chocolate-caramel soufflé he'd ordered at the beginning of the meal either. It was like the word *no* didn't exist for me tonight.

"Tell me about your research," he said after we'd eaten our meal and were waiting for the soufflé to be served since they were each made individually.

"Really?" I shook my head. "You'll be asleep before I finish explaining my dissertation."

"Try me."

"I've been studying how regulatory sequences control temporal and spatial patterns of gene expression by using a cDNA encoded reporter gene in transgenic mice. When I first started, the expression patterns we found were unexpected and that became the basis of my thesis…" I let my voice trail as I caught the glazed look he was trying valiantly to disguise. "Okay, too much. Basically, what I'm working on impacts the retina. Vision. Keeping people from going blind."

"Oh." He nodded. "That sounds amazing. How long until you get your PhD?"

"Good question. The research and data analysis are done, and I've finally gotten serious about writing the dissertation, so it's just a matter now of going back and forth with my mentor doing revisions and making it as good as I possibly can. I've got a date set to defend it in May."

"That's soon," he said, sounding surprised. "I don't know why. I thought it would take longer."

"I've been working toward this for a long time. The original goal was to be done by summer so I could move to Chicago and start my new life. Obviously, that's changed, but I'd still like to make the same deadline."

"What's next since you're not moving to Chicago?"

"Well, I still want to be done by summer," I said, chuckling. "Except now I don't have to search for a job in Chicago and can literally go anywhere."

"There's an interesting sense of freedom in that," he said thoughtfully. "Don't get me wrong. I love hockey, but it can be restrictive. I can only go where I'm offered a contract, you know?"

"Don't you like playing for the Mavericks?" I asked in surprise.

"I love the Mavericks. Truly. The town, my teammates, where I live. All of it. But there are other things that matter. Like family. This situation with Joey and my sister. And lots of other stuff we probably don't want to get into tonight. But I'll admit I'm a little envious of the ability to go anywhere you want."

"I still have to be offered a position," I countered. "Whether it's in a lab, or teaching, or something else. It's no different than any other job search, except now I don't have to restrict where I apply beyond whatever parameters I set for myself."

"Here you are." The waitress put a steaming soufflé down in front of us, and though I was still stuffed from dinner, my mouth watered.

"Jesus, that's decadent," I whispered.

"It is." Boone picked up the spoon and very slowly pushed it into the gooey creation between us. "Open up, gorgeous." He offered me the first bite and I parted my lips, waiting expectantly for the aromatic flavor to reach my taste buds.

"Oh fuck," I moaned. "That's...I'm not sure I can think of an adjective for how good that is."

"Wow, the PhD student at a loss for words," he teased, putting the spoon back in the soufflé. "Let's see what I can come up with." He took a bite and closed his eyes. He didn't react at first, merely taking his time as if savoring it. "Pales in comparison to tasting you," he said at last.

I swallowed, torn between wanting more dessert and the need to drag him out to the car and have my way with him right there in the parking lot.

Had any guy ever looked as good as Michael Boone did with a tiny drop of caramel dangling from his lips? Would it be gauche if I leaned over and licked it off?

"You have a little something on your…" I leaned over, using my fingers to gently wipe away the caramel. To my surprise, he turned his head, capturing my fingers with his lips and lightly sucking the tips.

"Mmm." His eyes met mine meaningfully, desire swirling in their depths.

I swallowed hard.

Oh yeah, this guy was going to rock my world.

"Maybe we should get going," I said.

Time momentarily froze as our eyes reflected the yearning in both of us.

Without breaking our gaze, he motioned for the check.

———

BOONE HELD my hand the whole drive back to my place. We didn't talk, but there didn't seem to be a need to. He gently rubbed his thumb along the skin of my hand, the light touch keeping me in a state of decadent arousal, reminiscent of that damn soufflé. Too much and not enough at the same time. I wanted more while simultaneously needing to be in the moment and enjoy whatever this was.

Boone kept an arm around my waist as we made our way up to my apartment and I turned to him the moment we locked the front door behind us. In my heels, we were just about eye level, and it was a heady feeling to be this close to him. Knowing what was coming.

"God, you're fucking beautiful," he said, the timbre of his voice making me tingle with anticipation. He caressed my cheek before leaning in, his lips seeking out mine.

On the inside, I was screaming with impatience and excitement, but my body followed his slower, more sensual lead. He wasn't in a hurry, his mouth taunting mine, his lips nipping and teasing. I melted into him, giving in to every crazy emotion he brought out in me. Normally, I kept myself in check, always needing to be in control. But not with Boone. I was going to throw caution to the wind tonight.

"Bedroom?" I murmured, unsure how much longer my legs would hold me up if he kept touching me.

"What's the rush?" he asked, smiling mischievously.

"My knees are weak," I admitted, chuckling.

He scooped me up in his arms and carried me

into my bedroom. "I plan to make your entire body weak before this night is over." He set me on the bed, raking his eyes up and down my body.

The only guy who'd ever been in my bedroom was Jarvis, and he'd done nothing but complain the whole time. How the bed was too small. How the bathroom was too cramped. How we could hear all the traffic from the nearby streets.

Boone didn't seem to be aware of anything but me.

As he gently took off my impossibly high heels and then stroked his hands along the arch of my foot and then up my calves.

As he pressed light kisses on my shins and the backs of my knees.

As he slid up my dress, running his hands along the insides of my thighs.

"Fucking perfect," he breathed, nuzzling my mound right through my black lace panties.

And still, he wasn't in a rush.

He kissed and nibbled and stroked me until I whimpered, digging my fingers into his hair. "Boone..."

"Let's get this off," he said, ignoring the plea in my voice.

I lifted my torso and he tugged my dress over my head, tossing it onto the floor and leaving me in nothing but my thong and strapless bra. He raked his eyes over me again, slowly. Methodically. As if memorizing every inch of me.

"I don't think I've ever seen anything so perfect." He dipped his head and tongued my belly button, his hands on either side of my hips. "Are you wet, Jolie?"

"God, yes."

"Let's see." He used his teeth to tug down my panties, a fraction of an inch at a time, his eyes on mine as he did it.

Even in the semidarkness, they were so fucking blue. They mesmerized me. *He* mesmerized me.

I moaned when he slipped a finger between my folds.

"I'm going to fuck you with my tongue first, Jolie," he said in a gruff voice. "And when you beg me to let you come, call me *Michael.*"

I couldn't do anything but groan because his mouth was right *there.* His tongue, his lips, torturing me into an even more heightened state of arousal. He used his fingers to spread me wide and then dove in. Slow, patient Boone was gone, replaced by ardent, voracious Michael.

And the only word that came to mind was heaven.

When he stabbed his tongue inside of me, my hips shot up off the mattress, arching into his face.

"Oh fuck, yes." I cried out, thrashing my head from side to side as I tried to hold out, make this last longer. It had only been a couple of minutes and I was so, so close.

"That's it, baby, ride my face," he growled against my overheated flesh.

"Michael…please!" I grabbed at his head, anxious to have him closer, deeper, all of him.

I felt fingers inside of me, teeth on my clit, and then there was nothing but a white-hot explosion of pleasure ricocheting through me like a gunshot.

"You're a squirter…" His rumbled comment barely permeated my haze of lusty satisfaction, but I felt wet and sated and out of control. "I fucking *love* that."

"Michael…" My voice was a whine as I clawed at his arms, unsure what I needed but desperate to get whatever it was.

"Right here, gorgeous." He slid up my body and I realized he was still mostly dressed, other than his shirt. "You ready for me to fuck you now?"

"So ready." I tugged his head down to mine, greedily sucking on his tongue, tasting myself on it and wondering why I'd never liked this before.

He barely broke away as he shimmied out of his slacks and fumbled with the condom.

"Hurry," I breathed. For some reason, one orgasm

wasn't enough. I needed him again, more, repeatedly. I didn't know what was wrong with me, but it felt incredibly important to have him inside of me.

Immediately.

"God…fuck…yes." He slid into me, bottoming out in one firm, reckless thrust.

"Oh. Wow." My eyes popped open as I stared at him.

One side of his mouth quirked up as he looked at me. "Wow?"

"You feel so good," I sighed happily. "Like you were made for me."

What the hell was I saying?

"I was thinking the exact same thing." He adjusted his hips and slowly pulled out to the tip. "Ready?" he asked.

"For?" I met his gaze curiously.

He reached for my hands, lifting them over my head and holding them with his, his eyes never leaving mine.

"Oh, baby…this is going to be so good." He kissed me, thrusting his tongue into my mouth as he slammed his hips against mine. My breath left me as he held me captive beneath him. It was incredibly freeing for him to be in control. I'd never felt like this before. And it was like he knew it. Like he knew exactly what I needed. Even better than I did.

I shifted restlessly as he began stroking into me, anxious for more.

"Michael…"

"I know, baby. Soon." He picked up speed, moving my hands together above my head so he could hold them with one hand. Then he used his free hand for balance as he pounded into me, all patience and teasing gone.

It was carnal and incredibly rough.

I was on the verge of detonating again, and he knew it.

"Squirt all over my cock, gorgeous," he growled against my mouth. "Now. Fucking come with me, Jolie."

His words were a direct hit to my libido and my body shot off without any input from my brain. I screamed and bucked and shook, as desperate to get out of his grasp as I was for him to never let go.

We rode our orgasms together, bodies moving in perfect sync, the roar that left him more primal than anything I'd ever heard.

"Michael." I whispered his name as he collapsed against me.

Holy fuck.

I was in so much trouble.

CHAPTER FIFTEEN

Boone

I woke the next morning to the savory smell of bacon mingled with the scent of freshly brewed coffee. Jolie's side of the bed was empty, and I blinked against the sunlight streaming in from an arched window on the wall to my right.

As I got up and put on the pants I'd left on her floor last night, I wished I didn't have to leave for practice. Last night had been the best first date of my life. We'd laughed, enjoyed a great meal and spent a couple of hours getting to know each other in bed. I wanted to do it again as soon as possible.

"Hey, good morning," I said, admiring the view of

her in nothing but a tank top and boxers as she poured a cup of coffee.

"Good morning," she said, flushing slightly.

"What's that for?" I asked, grinning.

She held out the cup of coffee, her brow furrowed. "It's for…you?"

"Not the coffee," I said as I took the mug. "But thank you. I meant the blush."

"Oh." She looked away, her cheeks a darker shade of pink now. "I was just thinking about last night."

I set the coffee down and put my hands on her hips, drawing her closer to me. As I leaned in, I said, "Tell me what you were thinking about."

Her breath hitched as I kissed her shoulder, slowly moving to her neck. She lifted her chin, giving me plenty of access.

"How can something that tickles also turn me on?" she asked lightly, her soft moan and warm skin making me hard.

I moved my hands higher, raising her tank top. She gasped as my fingers grazed the bottoms of her breasts.

"It's too bad I have to go," I said against her skin.

"What?" she squeaked.

"Yeah, I've got practice and I can't show up wearing last night's clothes."

She groaned with frustration. "That's not nice, getting me all worked up and then leaving."

"I never said I was nice."

I raised her top, baring her breasts and swiping my tongue over one of her nipples. She whimpered in response, trying to pull me closer.

"How long do you have?" she asked as I lifted her hips to ease her up onto the kitchen counter.

"What time is it?" I asked just before switching to her other nipple.

"Oh fuck…it's, uh…7:51."

"I've got about ten minutes."

The alarm I'd set on my phone sounded from the bedroom, and the smell of burning bacon filled the air, but neither of us could pull our attention from the other.

"That's enough," she said, unfastening my pants.

I laughed against her neck. "So I can go fuck myself on breakfast, then, is that it?"

"Right. You started this, now finish it."

Damn, I loved how assertive she was when it came to sex. She didn't hold back and act like my pleasure was all that mattered. Too many women did that. Nothing turned me on like a woman who wanted to give *and* get.

Jolie was panting with desire as I pushed my pants to the floor with one hand. It only took me a couple of seconds to get her boxers off, and then I buried myself inside of her, both of us groaning at the sensation.

She wrapped herself around me, her long legs tightly encircling my waist. I cupped her ass, lifting her off the counter and sliding her up and down my length, her cry of satisfaction sending a shot of arousal coursing through my veins.

"You love getting fucked, don't you, baby?" I said as I lowered her onto my shaft and then stopped. "Tell me how much you love it and I'll keep going."

She groaned, squirming against me in an effort to move herself up and down. It was futile, though. As she locked her gaze onto mine, she ran a hand into my hair and pulled on it, hard.

"I love the way you fuck me," she said, her voice so soft I barely heard the words. "Don't stop. Please."

"Damn, baby." I moved her up and then back down on my cock. "I'm going to fantasize every night about you saying those words."

Soon enough, she was squeezing my shoulders, frantically trying to move faster. I loved her desperation, but I also wanted to satisfy her, so I lifted her up and down faster, burying myself as deep as I could go. She was breathless, her skin flushed as she threw her head back and cried out.

"Oh fuck. Yes."

The sound of her coming and the feel of my cock soaked with her orgasm made me lose the last of my control, and I sank into her one last time, groaning hard as I emptied myself inside her.

Smoke filled the air, both of us realizing at the same time that we'd neglected the bacon for too long. As I set her down on the kitchen floor, the smoke alarm sounded, its shrill wail filling the apartment.

"Shit," she said, rushing over to turn off the stove burner. "My neighbors are going to kill me."

"Over your smoke detector going off?"

She waved a dish towel at the smoke as I moved the pan of blackened bacon to the other side of the stovetop.

"The smoke detectors in this building are interconnected," she said. "When one goes off, they all go off."

"Oh shit."

"Yeah." She grinned at me. "I probably shouldn't tell them what really happened."

As I watched her fan at the smoke with a worn dish towel, her tank top only covering the first couple of inches of her bare ass and her hair falling out of the loose bun she'd piled on top of her head, I felt a pang of something. I couldn't quite wrap my head around it, but it had something to do with this feeling good. With not wanting to leave. I had to shake it off, though, because practice started at nine.

"I'm sorry, I really do have to run," I said.

"It's okay. I have to get going soon, too."

She was waving the towel vigorously as I went into her bedroom to get the rest of my clothes and my shoes. I turned the alarm off on my phone, went into the bathroom to swish around some mouthwash so I could kiss her goodbye, and by the time I got back to the kitchen, the smoke alarm was off.

"Can we do this again as soon as possible?" I asked her.

"You mean the sex or the smoke alarm?"

I took her by the hips and pulled her close, both of us smiling. "I meant the date, smart-ass."

"Yes. I had an amazing time."

"Me too." I kissed her and she brushed the hair back from my forehead.

"But we need to keep things on the down-low when we're coaching youth hockey together. My dad's not ready to know I'm seeing someone else yet."

I sighed heavily, reminded that my attraction to Jolie had made me set aside my plans to stay on Coach's good side. He was going to kill me for this when he found out. But hopefully I could get traded before that happened.

"I'll do my best not to bend you over the wall at the rink during practices," I said with a mock sigh.

"How chivalrous."

I shrugged a shoulder and kissed her again. "I do what I can."

A pounding at Jolie's front door made her jump.

"Jolie! It's Marie! Are you home? We have to evacuate the building; the fire alarm went off!"

Jolie's eyes widened as she looked down at her near nakedness.

"Give me thirty seconds," she whispered.

She ran into her bedroom and emerged wearing sweats and a thick, oversized cardigan sweater, which she held closed with one hand.

"Jolie, are you in there?" the neighbor yelled. "I'm going to break the door down!"

"No, don't do that. I'm coming!" she said, running to unlock the door.

"Bye," I said, kissing the top of her head.

As she opened the door, her middle-aged neighbor looked back and forth between us.

"Didn't you hear the smoke alarm?" she said.

"Yeah, I'm so sorry, that was my fault," Jolie said. "I forgot I had bacon cooking and I got in the shower."

"You forgot?" her neighbor said skeptically.

I ducked my head and slipped out the door,

waiting until I'd gotten back to my car to laugh. The jokes about our smoking hot first date would write themselves.

———

A FEW HOURS LATER, we'd finished practice and a bunch of my teammates had gone out for lunch. We were meeting back up in our weight room later to lift. I was ravenous and had wanted to go to lunch with them, but something had held me back.

It was my teammate Sawyer. He was sitting alone in a corner of the locker room, and I knew why. I'd always remembered his late wife Annie's birthday because it was the same day as my dad's.

"Hey," I said, sitting down in a chair next to him once we were finally alone in the room. "You want to be alone, or is it okay if I sit?"

He seemed to snap out of his daze as he shrugged. "I don't care if you sit."

"My parents lost their first baby not long after she was born," I said. "My mom said her birthday was hard, but she wanted to do something every year to remember her anyway."

Sawyer nodded, a faraway look in his eyes. "It's hard not to think about what could've been. What should've been."

"I'm not going to hit you with clichés. But I'm here to listen if it helps."

He looked at me. "I appreciate it. I'm just thinking about all the birthdays I had with her. She always wanted to go out to the movies on her birthday. That was the only day she ate movie theater popcorn, even though she loved it. Annie never wanted a cake; she just wanted that popcorn."

He laughed softly, and I knew that while his physical self was in the locker room with me, in his heart, Sawyer was somewhere else, lost in his memories.

"Movie theater popcorn is the best," I said.

Sawyer scoffed, smiling sadly. "I didn't really get it, you know? I wish when we'd gone to those movies, I'd known we'd only get to do it as many times as we did. We didn't have much money when we were first together, so the movie and a new pair of shoes were about all we could afford for her birthday. But she was still so damn happy. Even when we had more money, Annie never changed, you know? I loved that about her."

"I remember her baking birthday cakes for all the guys who didn't have someone making them one. She'd make cakes for me and Kon every year, and you guys would have us over for dinner."

He smiled, tears shining in his eyes. "I haven't

thought about that in a long time. I'm glad you reminded me."

We sat in silence for a minute before I said, "Hey, you have plans tonight?"

"I never have plans, dude."

"Well, I've got my nephew Joey, so if you want, the three of us could go out for a movie. Have some dinner at the Olive Garden."

Sawyer sniffed and wiped the corner of his eye. "I can't believe you remember that was her favorite restaurant."

"Annie's not the kind of person you forget."

He looked away, probably so I wouldn't see him crying. Not that I cared, but I waited in silence until he'd composed himself enough to look at me again.

"I'd like that," he said. "We can see whatever movie Joey wants to see."

I stood up. "I'll text you and we'll pick you up on the way."

"Thanks, man."

I nodded and left him to remember Annie on his own. Grief had been a long, difficult road for him. For a while, he lay down right in the middle of the path and refused to move. At least now he was moving again, though he was on a path that would never truly end.

CHAPTER SIXTEEN

Jolie

I'D NEVER SEEN SO MUCH red. The first draft of my dissertation had come back to me looking like it had been through the aftereffects of a slasher movie. Exes and circles and so much red ink. Damn. This was the process. I understood that. I'd write and Dr. Matello would go through it with a fine-tooth comb, every time I turned it in, until we were both satisfied.

But damn, this first one was brutal.

I'd always been one of those kids who did well in school without having to kill myself. I understood the content of most of my classes without much effort, and that had continued into college.

Once I got to graduate school, it was second nature. Not that I didn't have to work hard, but I had the instinctive intelligence, especially in my chosen field, to be able to dig into the minutiae without being bogged down with commas and such.

Now I was going back to the drawing board and it burned my ass that Ellen was sitting at her desk smirking.

Bitch.

She'd probably added a few comments of her own.

"It's okay," Corrine whispered. "Everyone's first draft gets annihilated."

"Not mine," I grumbled under my breath, staring down at the papers in front of me.

Dr. Matello liked to do things old school, so I'd be printing everything out every time we did a draft. I thought it was a waste of paper, but he didn't like digital editing tools, so this was what I had to work with.

"It's going to be fine." I was surprised to feel Dr. Matello's hand on my shoulder, giving it a quick squeeze as he walked by. "Take it home, look at my comments, and then mull it over at hockey tonight. Tomorrow morning, you'll have a fresh perspective, and the next round will go more smoothly."

"Thank you." I nodded, grateful for his mentorship even when the criticism burned.

If I was honest, everything was more jarring today because I'd been away from all things academia for nearly a week, spending time with Joey, at hockey camp, and with Boone.

Boone.

My thoughts immediately drifted to last night.

It had been our second official date and we'd gone to the movies. So simple and spontaneous, yet somehow perfect. We'd chosen a new action movie, had the requisite argument about whether Marvel bested DC or vice versa, and then held hands like teenagers. Then we'd gone back to his place and he'd shown me a totally different kind of superhero.

I smiled just thinking about it, my hand drifting to the spot on my neck he seemed to focus on more than any other.

I'd seen him every day since that first night we'd slept together, even if it was only for a little while at hockey camp. We both had busy schedules, but he went out of his way to be attentive. A quick text, a wink from across the ice, something to let me know he was thinking about me. Jarvis had never been like that.

I stared down at the mass of papers in front of me, chewing my lip.

Maybe Dr. Matello had a point.

I should read his notes and then take the rest of the day to mull them over.

I was picking up Joey at five o'clock to go to hockey camp anyway, and I had errands to run as well as laundry to do. I probably could have spent the day helping Ellen, but my focus had begun to shift as I got closer to reaching the finish line of my PhD.

It was time to be selfish. I had to think about the next steps. Where I would do my postdoc work. If I truly wanted to leave St. Louis and my family. There were always opportunities at Johns Hopkins in New York, and one of my undergrad professors was there now, having extended an open invitation to visit anytime. I didn't know how I felt about the Big Apple, though. Sure, I loved a good weekend of Broadway shows, shopping, and great restaurants, but was I cut out for that hustle and bustle every day? The opportunities that came with a big-name university could change the trajectory of my career, but I was a Midwestern girl at heart.

Of course, it might be time to explore something different. I'd never lived outside of St. Louis, so maybe I had to think bigger.

I studied the first few pages of notes, frowning as I tried to figure out what changes I would make when I started editing. An insistent buzzing diverted my attention and I realized my phone was ringing.

"Hey, Hadley."

"Hey! I know it's a workday, but you said your schedule was flexible."

"Sure. What's up?"

"A few of us decided to take the kids to Chuck E. Cheese and I thought you might want to come."

I laughed. "Need an extra set of legs to chase them around?"

"Maybe." She laughed too. "But mostly it'll be a nice opportunity for girl talk while the kids are busy. Sheridan, Lucy, and our friend Nina are coming too."

I barely hesitated. "Sounds great. I'll meet you there."

"We're thinking around eleven thirty."

"See you then."

THE WELL-KNOWN children's entertainment center was fairly quiet today, so we squeezed into a couple of tables in the back. Hadley ordered pizza for the kids, passing out some tokens before watching them scatter. I'd never actually been here, though I knew lots of people who had, and it seemed like the perfect way to let kids burn off excess energy.

"I'm so tired of being pregnant," Sheridan moaned, resting her hands on her stomach. She was due fairly soon, though I didn't remember the exact date.

"Same." Hadley smiled. "But Wes is over the moon about the baby, and his excitement is so sweet. Makes me fall in love with him all over again."

"Not ready for that," Lucy said, shaking her head. "Kon and I are going to take the summer to explore Europe. Fifteen countries in six weeks."

"Holy shit," I breathed. "That sounds amazing."

"It's a little rushed, but the whole point is to see as many countries as possible. And we can adjust our schedule if we want to stay somewhere longer since we're driving for most of it."

"How exciting," I said. "I've never been out of North America. Europe is at the top of my list, though."

"Lars has it in his head we're taking the babies to Sweden this summer," Sheridan said, chuckling. "I don't think he has any idea what's about to happen to our lives. He's romanticized it in his mind."

"That's sweet, though," I said. "I mean, wouldn't it be worse if he didn't care at all?"

"Oh, for sure." Sheridan nodded. "He's been

amazing through the whole pregnancy, but I think he's looking at all our friends who've had one baby at a time, thinking we'll get some help and settle into a routine relatively quickly. The concept of two different babies, two different personalities, and potentially two totally different schedules hasn't sunk in."

Hadley grimaced. "I'm glad we're just having one, though the idea of being pregnant once and never again has its appeal."

"You think two babies are going to be enough for Lars?" Sheridan snorted. "He said he wants five."

"Five?" Lucy's eyes widened.

Then we all busted up laughing.

"Lord have mercy." Nina shook her head. "Let's revisit this conversation in six months."

"What about you, Jolie?" Lucy asked. "What's happening with your love life?"

My cheeks warmed.

I couldn't tell them about Boone and me.

Could I?

"Uh, nothing really. You know. I'm focused on writing my dissertation and helping out with Joey."

"Uh-huh." Sheridan cocked her head, a glint in her eye. "So you've learned how to give yourself hickeys?"

"What?" My hand immediately flew to my neck—

that damn place Boone loved to suck on—and the girls burst out laughing again.

"Who is it?" Hadley asked, leaning forward. "Come on, dish. I'm so married and pregnant, I have to live vicariously through you and Lucy."

My face had to be bright red. I couldn't tell them about Boone. If word got out, my father would lose his mind.

"I…can't," I whispered.

The four of them quickly got quiet, watching me intently.

"You're seeing someone on the team," Sheridan said slowly.

I didn't move. Hell, I could barely breathe.

"Boone." Lucy and Hadley spoke together.

I groaned.

"Why is it a secret?" Nina asked in confusion.

"You guys can't tell a soul," I said. "Please. You don't know my dad. He can be such a jerk when it comes to me and this is Boone's career. His livelihood. It could go wrong in so many ways."

"Your dad would do something like that?" Sheridan asked.

"Not directly, but yes, he could make his life miserable for no reason other than he's my dad and the only guys good enough for me are the ones he picks. Please. Promise me that this stays between us."

"You can trust us," Hadley said firmly.

"Not even to the guys," I said firmly, looking around.

Sheridan held out her pinkie. "Pinkie swear, ladies. Then we get the deets."

All five of us awkwardly locked our pinkies together and then Hadley leaned forward. "Now. Details."

I chuckled. "Look, honestly, the biggest reason I don't want word to get out is that this is just casual. We're having a good time. He's got this situation with Joey and I'm trying to finish my PhD, so it's been nice to have someone to talk to. For both of us."

Lucy looked skeptical. "You realize that's what we all say, right? It's casual. It's just sex. I don't know where it's going. Friends with benefits. Oh, it's no big deal. Those are literally the lies we tell ourselves when we're in denial."

"I don't even know if I'm staying in St. Louis," I said slowly. "I'm assuming I'm going to get my PhD by summer, but then I have to find a postdoc job and it's probably not going to be here. In fact, I'm thinking of interviewing at Johns Hopkins in New York City."

They all stared at me.

"And you guys know how hockey is," I continued. "Boone could get traded anytime. Then what would we do? How would that work? So in our case, it's exponentially complicated by my work."

"Love is always complicated."

"Seriously, it's been two dates," I protested. "Love isn't anywhere on our radar."

"Famous last words," Nina murmured.

"But the sex is good if you're letting him leave you love bites," Sheridan teased, her eyes gleaming.

"The sex is…really good." We could talk about sex. Feelings were a lot messier, but sex was easy.

"Don't dismiss a guy who rocks your world in bed," Hadley said. "Sex isn't everything, but it's hard to find a guy who knows what he's doing."

"That's for sure," Nina said, nodding.

"I'm going to have to wear a scarf on Sunday," I moaned. "My dad will spot a hickey a mile away."

"I'll text you the name of a concealer that's like magic," Sheridan said. "It'll cover it right up."

"Thanks."

"Coach Jolie, will you play air hockey with me?" Joey came running up to me, his eyes bright with excitement.

Thank god.

"Sure." I got to my feet and let him take my hand. "Duty calls," I said as he dragged me away.

It was fun to have girl talk but also a little scary because these women all knew Boone. If they told their husbands about us, word might get out and I really didn't want him to be the focus of my father's ire. And I had no doubt Dad would be spectacularly unhappy if he found out I was dating one of the Mavericks, even though I was happier than I'd ever been.

CHAPTER SEVENTEEN

Boone

"You have to cycle the puck back." Coach Gizzard pushed a button on his remote, freezing the video on the TV screen in the Chicago training room. "You see, right there. That's a missed opportunity."

I nodded and glanced at Nash, who was grimacing. Our five-man first line was in a pregame meeting with Coach Gizzard, reviewing film before tonight's game. The missed opportunity Coach had just pointed out had been Nash's, and Nash didn't make many mistakes.

Being on the first offensive line with Wes and Nash carried a lot of pressure. They were both exceptional players. I'd worked my way up to the first line, and I often wondered how long I'd be able to sustain playing at this level. After this meeting, I had to get my hand iced because it was sore from getting boarded hard in a home game the night before last.

"Hudson consistently does this," Coach said, now talking about one of the Chicago players so we could hopefully take advantage of his weakness in tonight's game.

I was still listening, but my mind was wandering. To Jolie, because this was the first day since our first date that we wouldn't get to see each other, and to Joey, for several reasons.

He'd gotten to talk to Emma on the phone yesterday, and it had been a mixed bag. He was thrilled to hear her voice, but he'd hit her hard with questions about why she couldn't come get him. The hurt in his little voice had gotten to me; I could only imagine how hard it had been for my sister.

Fifteen days in and she was doing well, but she missed her kid. She'd stayed strong while talking to him but broke down when it was just me on the phone. I'd assured her he was in the best of hands, and then I'd had to leave again today.

Joey had begged me to stay. He had a good time over at Wes and Hadley's, but that didn't make me feel any better when he was crying for me not to go.

"There's not one reason we shouldn't dominate this game," Gizzard said. "Dominate. Especially with Stanton on the IR."

Mike Stanton, Chicago's star player, was on injured reserve with a pulled groin. In the back of my mind, I was hoping to put Jarvis there with him. The more Jolie told me about how he'd treated her, the more I disliked him. If I started shit with someone for no good reason tonight, just to get them out of their zone, it would be him.

"Questions?" Coach asked.

I shook my head and looked around at the other guys, who were all silent. Coach Gizzard seemed more intense than usual today, like he wanted a win badly. It was probably because we needed a win to put us back in first place, but there was something more to it, too.

We used to joke, quietly of course, that Gizzard was pulling for Chicago when we played them since Jarvis was the son he never had. Not anymore, though.

Coach Gizzard was a great coach. He was deliberate about letting his players know we could come to him with personal issues if we needed time off, but he didn't want us to consider him a friend. He'd given up on his hair, which was slowly disappearing, last year and started shaving his head. That was the kind of man he was—a straight shooter. He often used the lipstick and pig analogy. It took a lot to coach at this level of the game, and he never asked more of any of us than he asked of himself as far as time spent in the arena. I respected him a lot.

"Boone, can you stay behind for a minute?" he asked as he ended the meeting.

"Sure, Coach."

"Ron, tell the second liners I'll be ready in ten minutes," he said to one of our assistant coaches, who nodded and closed the door behind him.

I sat back down in the metal folding chair I'd been watching film in, my heart pounding. The deadline for trades was approaching, and based on Evelyn's informal inquiries, Coach Gizzard had to know I wanted to go to Nashville.

This could be it. He could be telling me tonight was my last game with St. Louis. I was relieved before he even said a word at the thought of taking Joey home while Emma completed her treatment. We'd finally be with family, which I needed more than ever. I had no experience dealing with a kid crying because I was leaving, not to mention the trauma he was experiencing over Emma being gone. I'd hire someone to help with him when I needed it, but I knew we'd be okay. When Emma finished treatment, she could move in with me.

I'd miss Jolie, but my family needed me. If Andy was nearing the end of his life, I had to be there for him as much as possible.

"I'll get right to the point," Coach said. "I hear my daughter is spending a lot of time taking care of your kid."

Record scratch.

"I don't have a kid, Coach. Joey's my nephew."

He glared at me. "Whatever he is, why is my daughter, who is supposed to be working on her dissertation, taking him to Chuck E. Cheese and out to lunch with my mother?"

I didn't have the fiery temper a lot of my teammates did. I considered myself damn lucky to even be on a professional team, and I kept my head down and did my part. But hearing Coach talk about Joey with derision in his voice, like he wasn't worthy of Jolie's attention, set me off in an instant. I took a second, forcing myself not to fly off the handle like I wanted to.

"Jolie has become friends with a lot of the wives, and she offered to help Hadley Kirby with Joey when I'm on the road. He's with me the rest of the time because my sis"

His eyes widened and his engine light came on. That's what we called it when Coach Gizzard's neck vein bulged—it meant he was really pissed.

"I don't give a good goddamn why he's with you! I asked you why you're using my daughter as your babysitter. That's the only question you need to answer."

Asshole. Why did I respect this man who didn't give a shit about me or my family?

"I never asked her to do it," I said, sitting up to my full height and holding his gaze. "She offered."

"And that's when a light should go off in that tiny little brain of yours reminding you that I told you to stay the fuck away from my daughter!"

Nash would tell him to go fuck himself. He wouldn't worry about the consequences. But I couldn't. I needed my job, and I needed a trade. I couldn't help getting in a small jab, though.

"Well, Coach, if Jolie is taking care of Joey while I'm on the road, I'm not actually near her."

I thought the vein was going to explode. He tossed his remote to the other side of the room and it silently hit the wall and slid down. Our video coordinator Mo had wrapped the remote in bubble wrap and duct tape, leaving only the buttons exposed for such occasions.

"Don't get cute with me, Boone! I know what you're doing. You're using that kid to get into my daughter's pants and so help me"

I stood up, my throat tight. "With all due respect,

go to hell, Coach. My nephew has been through more than you can imagine, and he's *four fucking years old*. This isn't about you."

Angry tears blurred my vision as I pictured Joey clutching the stuffed elephant that was the only constant in his life. Coach Gizzard could talk all the shit he wanted about me, but I wouldn't listen to him telling me Joey was unworthy or a pawn in some grand scheme to get laid.

"I could have phrased that better," Coach said, backpedaling a little and looking contrite. "The point is, you care about your family and I care about mine. My daughter's been through a lot, too. She's been in college for…hell, I think eight years now, and she's finally finishing. She's our only child."

The vein was receding. He was actually trying to be decent about this. I took a deep breath, taking the same tone.

"She's an amazing woman. You should be very proud of her. And I'd never do anything to get in the way of her school. Jolie volunteers to help with Joey. She likes being part of the group. You know, the players and wives. Everyone likes her."

He narrowed his eyes. "I've seen you looking at her, Boone. You seem to like her more than everyone else."

Our eyes remained locked as a few tense seconds

of silence passed. I wasn't going to deny it because I wasn't a coward or a liar. Coach didn't seem to get that his daughter was gorgeous, warm, and smart—every man who saw her probably wished she were his.

"There's one obvious solution to this," I said.

He scoffed. "It'll be a cold day in hell when I give you my blessing to date my daughter."

His words hit me like a physical blow, but I didn't let it show. I wasn't a womanizer or an asshole. He made me out to be some nightmare of a boyfriend, and I didn't deserve that.

"That's not what I meant," I said, my tone cold. "You know I want a trade to Nashville. Just trade me and I'll be out of your hair."

He exhaled hard. "You know that's not just my decision."

"You've got the power to make it happen and we both know it."

I was pretty sure he would have thrown the remote again if it was within arm's reach.

"I can't trade one of my first-line players when we're tied for first place in the standings," he said, his tone weary. "But I'll make you a deal. Stay away from my daughter—both you and your nephew—and at the end of the season, you'll get your trade."

I shook my head. "I need it sooner."

He didn't give a shit about my brother or his illness, so I didn't bother going into it. I actually felt protective of my family after the way he'd talked about Joey. He didn't deserve to know the details of why I wanted the trade.

"Why?" he asked.

"That's my business."

"Did you get someone in Nashville pregnant?"

I wanted to quit hockey on the spot and walk out of the room because fuck him. I didn't sleep with every willing woman I met, unlike some of my teammates. Coach was just hell-bent on being an asshole to me.

I couldn't quit, though. The money I made would take care of everyone in my family. Andy, Carrie, and Mason. Emma and Joey. My mom. I wouldn't let my pride get in the way of their security.

"Does it matter why I want the trade?"

He looked smug. "That's it, isn't it? You've got a baby on the way."

How had someone as sweet and warm as Jolie been raised by this guy? I'd lost all respect for my coach in a matter of five minutes. Only my closest friends on the team knew about my brother, and none of them would ever repeat my business.

I hated that I had to rely on Gizzard for my trade, but I did. He had the power to make or break me, which meant he had the power to make or break my family.

"Okay, deal," I said, not even looking at him again as I turned and left the room.

My stomach was knotted in anger. I really liked Jolie, and I wanted to keep seeing her for as long as I could. But I was going to Nashville at the end of the season, and she could end up anywhere.

I had to make a sure move.

"Hey," I said to Wes when I caught up with him. "Will you ask Hadley to make sure Joey stays with her for this whole road trip? She can have your nanny help. I'll pay her."

He furrowed his brow. "Yeah, I'll do that. What's up?"

I shook my head. "I can't tell you right now. I just need Hadley to keep him until I get home and can hire my own nanny to help out."

"Dude, you don't need to do that. Between Hadley, Jolie, and Sheridan"

I put a hand out to stop him. "I'll tell you about it later. For now, just trust me."

He nodded. "Of course. I'll text Had right now."

"Thanks."

We had about thirty minutes of downtime before our pregame skate, but I couldn't even look at my phone. I had a feeling there would be a text from Jolie, and I couldn't bear to see it.

I liked her. Really liked her, more than I'd liked anyone in a long time. But I had no choice. I had to stop seeing her.

CHAPTER EIGHTEEN

Jolie

I SPENT all day Saturday working on revisions for my dissertation, trying to keep distractions to a minimum. I hadn't heard from Boone in a couple of days, and though I understood he was busy with hockey, I knew from experience there was a lot of downtime on the road. A tiny part of me wondered if I'd been too forward with him or if I'd been nothing but a convenient sex partner since I'd been so involved in helping with Joey.

That line of thinking just pissed me off, though.

Boone could sleep with anyone. From what I'd heard through the grapevine, he did sleep with anyone and everyone. He didn't have to sleep with his coach's daughter, especially when my father would undoubtedly be furious if he found out.

So what the hell was going on?

I itched to call and ask him, but I also didn't want to be that girl, the one who chased a guy who didn't want to be caught. I'd played that game in the past, and it just made me feel bad about myself.

I'd thought this thing with Boone and I was different, that *he* was different, but now I wasn't sure. Technically, I was on the rebound, so it hadn't occurred to me that I might start to feel something for him. Something that went beyond mind-blowing sex and a mutual love for Joey. The truth was that I'd never loved Jarvis, so there really hadn't been a mourning period or any emotional pain to get past. I'd been ready for something—someone—new.

It made no sense that he would blow me off without a word, and there was no way he was that busy. The guys had tons of time on the road, especially when they were on planes and buses.

I decided to text him before I left for my parents' house for dinner.

JOLIE: Hey. Just wanted to say hi. I haven't heard from you in a few days. Everything okay?

He didn't respond, so I changed into jeans and a sweater and headed out. I'd put in eight hours editing and reworking my dissertation, so it would be good to spend the evening with Mom and Grandma G.

I picked up Grandma on the way and we chatted as I drove.

"I feel like I should move to an island in the Caribbean," she said. "Somewhere warm and sunny and on the beach."

"What about hurricanes?" I asked.

She shrugged. "You gotta go sometime, right? Live a wonderful, relaxed life on the beach and die happy, or stay here and freeze to death."

I laughed. "You have a lovely, warm apartment. What's up with this sudden need for change?"

"I'm old but not dead. And I'm in a rut. I need an adventure."

I glanced over at her. "Then go on a cruise. I'd be sad if you moved away."

"You were going to move to Chicago." She pointed out.

"I don't know that I was," I admitted. "I know that was the plan, but somehow, deep down inside, I'm not sure I believed the wedding would ever happen. I think there was part of me waiting for him to dump me so I wouldn't have to deal with my father. When he didn't, I had to do something drastic."

"It was certainly drastic."

"I've been dating Michael Boone," I blurted out.

"Well. Now it all makes sense."

"What makes sense?" I asked, frowning.

"Your father was on a tear the other day. I was over at the house and he was talking to your mom about you and Jarvis, asking her what she thought he should do to get the two of you in the same room together."

I groaned. "Seriously?"

"I'd nodded off on the couch, so they thought I was asleep. Your mother suggested he not do anything until after you defended your dissertation, but your dad said that would be too long, that Jarvis wouldn't wait forever."

"He's going to have to," I muttered.

"Well, your dad said something like, 'she's academically brilliant but has no idea about men. We have to do something to make sure she's taken care of by the right guy.' I almost snorted but managed not to since then I wouldn't be able to eavesdrop anymore."

That sounded like something my father would say. "You think he knows about me and Boone?"

"He must have an inkling. He sounded desperate to get you and Jarvis back together."

"I guess now I know what's going on." I tightened my grip on the steering wheel, annoyance washing over me.

"What?"

"He's gone radio silent. Boone, I mean. Which means Dad got to him."

"You don't know that for sure, so let's not jump to any conclusions."

"There's no doubt in my mind. Jarvis still calls me a couple of times a week, even though I never pick up, so I'm sure Dad is hounding him to keep trying while simultaneously doing something to scare Boone off. Dammit."

"I love my son, but he's standing on my last nerve," Grandma G said, her voice laced with irritation.

"Tell me about it."

"Do you like him?"

"Who? Boone? Of course. He's…amazing."

"Then don't let your father do this to you. Take control of your life, Jolie. That's why you walked out on your wedding, right? So you wouldn't be forced to settle for a man you weren't in love with. If you think Boone will make you happy, fight for it. Fight for him."

"But at what cost? He's trying to get traded to Nashville, and Dad can prevent it. I don't want to be the reason he's stuck here. Then he'd resent me."

"He's leaving the team?" Grandma sounded surprised. "But why?"

"I don't know for sure. Something about family

being there. We, uh, well, we haven't talked about any of that stuff. It's been casual, you know? We've been getting to know each other. I figured we had time until we had to worry about the future."

"You know better than anyone how stubborn your father can be. If he got wind of what's going on…" She lifted a shoulder.

I did know how stubborn Dad was.

But there was something he'd apparently forgotten.

I was his daughter, and my own stubborn streak was a mile long.

———

BOONE DIDN'T RESPOND to my text the next day either and I was pissed. If he truly didn't want to see me anymore, that was okay, but he should have been man enough to tell me to my face. The team was coming home tonight, though, and I planned to be at Hadley's when he got there to pick up Joey. I could understand his hesitance to get in touch if my father had somehow intimidated him professionally, but the more I thought about it, the angrier I got. And I refused to be manipulated again. I'd allowed my father to set me up with Jarvis because I'd been too buried in schoolwork to give it much thought.

I'd never let that happen again.

I was going to have a conversation with Boone and then, depending on what he said, my father and I were going to have a heart-to-heart as well. I loved my father, but he was gruff, opinionated, and often completely self-absorbed. It was his way or the highway, and while my mom had always been a bit of a buffer between us growing up, I wasn't a little girl anymore. I didn't need anyone to fight my battles.

"You okay?" Hadley asked me after Joey, Annalise, and Benny had gone to bed. "You've been quiet tonight."

"Sorry." I scooped up a handful of sippy cups that had been abandoned in the playroom. "Just a lot on my mind."

"Boone?"

"Among other things." I absently rinsed the cups and put them in the dishwasher.

"Jarvis?"

"What?" I turned in surprise. "What makes you say that? I think about him as little as possible."

"I don't know. Rumor has it you're talking again."

"Rumor has it? What rumor? My father's wishful thinking?"

Hadley grimaced. "I don't know. Wes mentioned he'd heard it somewhere."

I was truly going to kill my father.

"My dad can be very single-minded, but he seems to forget that I'm an adult. I try not to be confrontational with him because he yells and his face turns red and then he storms out, which upsets my mother. It's a whole thing in our house, which is why I live in an apartment even though it would be cheaper to live at home. He's gotten worse as he's gotten older. It makes him a great coach, I think, but not the best husband or father."

"That must be hard for you," she said gently.

"You have no idea. And the worst part is, I have so many great memories of when I was little. Him teaching me to skate, play hockey, shoot baskets, all the things he would have taught a son. Until one day I became a young woman and it was like someone flipped a switch on our relationship. At that age, around thirteen, most of us are totally self-absorbed, between school and boys and all that goes with adolescence, so it wasn't until college that I realized how far apart we'd drifted. When he shoved Jarvis in my face, I felt like this would be the thing that would repair our relationship."

"And now?"

"Now it's the thing that's going to drive me batshit crazy."

"What are you going to do?"

"I have to talk to him. Try to make him understand how miserable Jarvis made me, and maybe get him to lay off Boone. If he refuses, then it might be time to play hardball."

"Which is what?" Hadley asked, concern on her face.

"Essentially cutting him off." I smiled wryly. "Dad's really protective of our family unit. Sunday dinners. Time with Grandma G. Things like that. If I stop participating, it will fuck with the whole dynamic. Then my mother will be pissed, and once she's pissed, his life becomes difficult. I hate playing games, but he has to stop interfering in my life. It's as simple as that."

"Well, I don't know that I can do anything to help, but I'm always here if you need a friend."

"Thank you. I appreciate that more than you know."

"Of course." Hadley looked up at the sound of the garage door opening. "Sounds like Wes is home, which means Boone is probably right behind him."

I nodded. "I'm going to meet him outside so we can talk for a few before he gets Joey. Is that okay?"

"Do what you need to do. I can have Wes carry Joey out if necessary."

"Thanks." I grabbed my jacket and walked out the front door.

Sure enough, Boone was just getting out of his SUV and he glanced up as I approached.

"Hey." He didn't look surprised to see me.

"Hi." I walked over to him and stopped a foot or so away, lifting my chin as I met his gaze. "You and I need to talk."

CHAPTER NINETEEN

Boone

THIS WAS the last thing I needed. Jolie was approaching my car, her long, fiery hair whipping around her head from the wind. And she looked pissed.

Rightfully so. I'd been blowing her off since Coach's offer of a deal, and I didn't want to lie to her about it. This was the price I had to pay for giving in to my attraction to her. I'd known from the beginning that I couldn't have it all.

"Don't you have the balls to say it to my face?" she asked when she reached me.

I looked away because she was right. But also, she wasn't. It was never my plan to not see her again. I just needed to secure this trade first. And then? Well, it would depend on where she ended up finding a job.

"There's nothing to say right now," I said. "I've been on the road. I should have texted you back."

She scoffed. I could practically see her temperature rising, her face flushed with anger. It looked a lot like her expression just before coming, actually, and it was damn sexy.

Shit. This wasn't a good time to get turned on. I'd slept like shit on the road trip and my left shoulder was killing me from a hard hit I took. I just wanted to get Joey, go home, and forget the way my coach was holding me hostage.

"Is this how you treat women after you've slept with them?" She crossed her arms, her eyes narrowed into murderous slits. "Is the novelty of me gone now?"

I met her gaze, hating that she would ever think that. "That's not it, Jolie. Things are complicated."

"Not really. Let me guess, my dad talked to you, didn't he? Did he get all high and mighty and stomp around like a moody toddler?"

I shrugged, trying to play it cool. "That must be where you get it."

She approached and tried to shove me with a palm, but my feet stayed planted and I didn't move.

"Don't you dare make fun of me right now," she said.

"I'm not making fun of you. I just..." My gaze dropped to my feet.

"Just be honest with me." Her voice broke. "Is it my dad, or is it something else?"

I looked up at her, guilt stabbing my chest over her wondering if I just didn't like her anymore. That was so far from the truth. She was the reason I hadn't slept on the road trip. I'd finally found someone who had it all—sexy, smart, caring, funny —and I couldn't have her.

"Yeah, it's him," I confessed. "He has a lot of control over my life."

She shook her head, tears shining in her eyes. "He told you he won't give you the trade because of me, didn't he?"

Frustration welled inside me. I wanted to punch something. I didn't deserve to be treated this way by Coach, but Jolie deserved it even less. This was her own father, sabotaging her happiness so he could get what he wanted.

I gently tipped her chin up until our gazes locked. "I don't just want that trade, okay? I *need* it. I have to have it. My brother..." I cleared the emotion from my throat. "He has cancer. And he has a family. We don't know how this is going to play out after this round of treatment, but my family means more to me than anything else. Much more than hockey."

The fire in her eyes went out, replaced by concern. She blinked and tears ran from the corners of her eyes.

"Boone, I'm so sorry."

"It's"

"No, listen to me." She put both palms on my chest and leaned in close. "I want to apologize to you on behalf of my dad. He's not a bad person, but he's way too stubborn. And if you need that trade and he knows why"

"He doesn't."

Her expression softened. "Maybe you should tell him."

Damn. This woman really was one in a million. She wasn't thinking about herself at all. Her concern was for me. For my brother. And still, she believed her dad was capable of doing the right thing.

I wanted to believe it, but I knew Coach had to consider more than just my personal life. The Mavericks were still in playoff contention, and he had to keep his team stacked with the best players who had the most chemistry. Otherwise, he risked losing his job and his reputation as a coach.

"My brother's a private person," I said. "Don't tell

anyone what I told you. If news gets out that I'm trying to get traded and that's why…"

She nodded. "Reporters will come knocking on his door. That's the last thing he needs."

I gave in to the pull I felt, putting my hands on her hips and leaning my forehead against hers. "I missed you."

Her breath hitched. "I missed you, too. And I'm sorry I assumed…anything. I'm sorry for not just talking to you about it."

"No, this is on me. I like you a lot and…I hope you still like me?"

She hummed a note of laughter. "You're okay I guess."

"If this was just about what I wanted, you and I would be in the back of my car right now, fogging up the windows."

Her fingertips pressed against my chest as she grabbed two handfuls of my shirt. "Really?"

"Oh yeah." I tilted my head to the side and kissed her softly. "You're all I thought about on the road. I'm wound so tight, and I just want to work that long, sexy body of yours until we're both exhausted."

She laughed lightly against my lips. "You've taken a dramatic turn over the past five minutes. I thought you were done with me."

I slid my arms around her waist and she melted

into me, neither of us seeming to feel the ice-cold wind around us. Just this—having her in my arms—made everything feel right again.

"I thought about things a lot on my road trip," I said. "And I need a few days to talk to my agent and my financial planner, so keep this between us, but… if it comes down to it, I'm prepared to leave the team and retire."

She pulled back, pressing her hands against my chest and giving me an incredulous, open-mouthed look.

"Quit hockey?"

I nodded. "It might not be forever. Maybe it will be. I don't know. I just know, deep down, that if my brother doesn't make it, I'll never look back and wish I'd devoted more time to hockey. I play for a coach that doesn't give a shit about me. My teammates will be part of my life forever, whether we still play together or not."

Jolie looked stunned. "But you've worked so hard to get here."

I shrugged. "And it's been good to me. I'm pretty sure I've got enough money to take care of my family and that's all I really need."

She wiped a tear from the corner of her eye. "You've got my support, no matter what. I know this thing between us can't last. It's just…timing, I guess."

She was right. Not only was she fresh off of a broken engagement, but I wasn't planning to stay in St. Louis, one way or another, and soon she'd be applying for jobs all over the place. It was unfair that I'd met the best possible woman at the worst possible time.

"Well, listen," I said, brushing a strand of hair back from her face. "I'm out of here at the end of this season, either through a trade or because I'll quit. So why don't we make the most of the time we have together?"

She smiled playfully. "Are you going to suggest the back of the car thing again? Wes and Hadley might have something to say about that."

"Yeah, because they're jealous," I said, winking.

"Maybe we could meet up for lunch tomorrow," she said.

Tomorrow was so damn far away. I wanted her now. Here. Everywhere. Hard. Slow. Fast. But it wasn't in the cards.

"Yeah, I guess I have to get Joey," I said, coming back down to earth.

"He tried so hard to stay awake until you got here."

I'd missed him, too. I was used to him asking me at least two hundred questions a day, and life on the road without him was too quiet.

"He didn't make it?"

She shook her head. "We watched a movie and had hot chocolate, then drew pictures. He practically fell asleep in his coloring book."

"Thanks for hanging out with him. He really likes you."

"I like him, too." She broke out in a grin, her eyes sparkling happily. "You want to hear something funny?"

"Always."

"Benny can't pronounce your name right. He hears Joey talking about you, so he talks about you, too, but he calls you Uncle Poon."

"Oh shit." I cringed and laughed at the same time. "Wait until Wes hears him say that. They'll literally never refer to me as anything else in the locker room again."

"Just don't ask me to call you that in bed."

I kissed her once, softly, and then again. It was so damn hot finding a woman who was smart and quick and funny. She didn't just make eyes at me and laugh at everything that came out of my mouth. Jolie and I were equals. Well, close enough, anyway. She was probably smarter than me if I was being real about it, but I wasn't exactly a slacker.

"Come on home with Uncle Poon," I teased. "I'll make you feel real good."

"Oh my god. I cannot." She shook her head and laughed. "Don't bring this up over lunch tomorrow."

"Speaking of lunch…it's not going to be a sex lunch because I'll have Joey."

I kept forgetting about my little cockblocking nephew. Wes and Hadley scheduled sex—it was actually in her planner and on their shared online calendar, and now I understood why.

"Oh, right." She shrugged. "Well, there's always Chuck E. Cheese and some under-the-table groping."

I arched my brows at her in appreciation. "Are you offering to give me a handy at Chuck E. Cheese, Miss Gizzard?"

"Jesus, no. I'd like to not get arrested, thanks. Just some over-the-clothes…affection, we'll call it."

"Overpriced shitty cheese pizza and possibly having my dick brushed through my pants." I feigned excitement. "Awesome."

"Got a better idea?"

I kissed her on the forehead. "It actually sounds fun, babe. Joey accused me of sucking at the basketball toss last time we were there, and I need to show him what's up."

"Tomorrow, then." She gave me a quick kiss. "Now let's go inside. My hands are numb."

I put my arm around her as we took the sidewalk

that led to Wes and Hadley's front door. I'd been planning to keep the plan I had in my back pocket—quitting hockey—to myself, but it was nice to have a woman in my life I trusted enough to share it with.

Best woman. Worst timing.

CHAPTER TWENTY

Jolie

THE NEXT SET of revisions wasn't quite as bad as the first, but it was still a lot of red ink. I stared at the papers in front of me, trying to decide if it was too late in the day to start working on edits. It was after three and I had to be at the rink at five. Boone and my dad would be there too, so Boone and I were going to have to cool it, which pissed me off all over again.

We'd seen a lot of each other in the last couple of weeks. He was a great guy who made me happy, so I resented having to sneak around. I hadn't had a chance to confront my father yet, so that didn't help.

I needed him to understand that he couldn't play with people's lives. Especially not because of me.

Michael Boone, the man, was nothing like Boone, the hockey player. He was thoughtful and insightful, cared deeply about family, and always made me feel like I was the most important thing in his life when we were together. Joey was his priority right now, of course, but Boone made sure I knew he was thinking about me. There wasn't a lot of alone time, but we made the most of it when it happened.

Revisions could wait, I decided, putting the papers in my backpack after I cleaned up my desk. I hadn't been at the lab much lately, spending the bulk of my time writing and editing and rewriting my dissertation. I usually worked at home, but I'd also been spending time at Boone's with him and Joey. We had a lot of fun together.

Joey was such a sweet kid; I was going to miss him when he and Boone moved to Nashville.

I was going to miss Boone more though.

He'd become extremely important to me in a very short time, so it was difficult to imagine my life going back to the way it had been before we'd started dating. And dating other guys? That would be impossible. The very thought made me shudder with revulsion.

I was headed for a broken heart; I already knew this.

But Boone and Joey were worth it.

That was the only justification I had for allowing myself to feel things I shouldn't be feeling.

Until his mother was out of rehab, Joey needed all the love and attention we could shower on him. Whether it was Boone, me, or the extended Mavericks family, we were doing everything in our power to get him through this. Beyond that, once Boone was gone, I'd throw myself into my work. That was the one thing that would keep me from falling apart.

The arena seemed busier than usual, and I had to park all the way in the back. I couldn't imagine what was going on, on a random Thursday afternoon, but there were people everywhere.

The reason for the fuss was evident the moment I walked into the rink, and I couldn't stop the sigh that left me.

"Did you know about this?" Jana whispered to me as I watched the crowd of people surrounding Jarvis.

Of course Jarvis was here.

The Mavericks were playing Chicago tomorrow night, so he'd come into town early to make my life miserable. Most likely at my father's request.

"You think I'd be here if I'd known about this?" I muttered.

"Coach Jolie!" Joey's little voice made me smile despite this frustrating new development.

"Hey, kiddo." I turned and squatted down onto my haunches, holding out my arms. This was how we always greeted each other lately, and he launched himself at me. Boone was a few feet behind him, and his eyes moved to Jarvis, narrowing slightly.

Great.

The last thing we needed was a scene between him and Jarvis. Or worse, between him and my dad.

"Don't," I said to him in a soft voice as he approached. "Just ignore him."

"You sure you don't want him, Jolie?" Jana asked, ignoring Boone and staring at Jarvis with wide eyes. "Because I'd ride him like a fucking bronco."

"Have at it," I said, shrugging. "He's only good for about three minutes, though, so make sure you're quick."

Boone snorted out a laugh as he scooped up Joey and headed for the men's locker room.

"Why do you have to crush my dreams like that?" Jana moaned, laughing.

"Just telling the truth. Come on. Let's hit the locker room and put our skates on."

"I have to get mine sharpened," Jana said. "But I'll see you out there."

"Okay." I headed for the women's locker room when I heard my name being called.

Goddamn it.

I couldn't ignore him because there were people everywhere and there was no doubt that the masses were taking video of everything he did.

"Hey, Jarvis." I turned, hoping I had a neutral look on my face.

He leaned over and brushed his lips across my cheek.

"Don't do that," I hissed under my breath.

"Come on, don't be this way. Can we talk?"

"No."

He sighed, shaking his head. "Why do I even bother? You're so damn stubborn."

"You really thought doing this here, in front of all these kids and their parents, was a good idea?"

"Your dad and I figured you'd be more comfortable here than if I showed up unannounced at your apartment."

"Well, at least you were right about something."

"Can we have dinner or lunch or something? Please?"

"Jarvis, listen. This is a lesson in futility. I've moved on and so should you. I'm going to defend my dissertation soon and I've been applying for jobs all over the country. I don't know what's going to happen with any of it, but I do know that you and I were not meant to be. We're too different."

He scowled. "Is it about the prenup?" he asked suddenly.

"What?" He'd asked me to sign one about a month before the wedding, and I hadn't hesitated.

"We can tear it up," he said. "I don't care about the money."

"I was never interested in your money," I said, keeping my voice level. "And if you really loved me, you'd know that about me."

"I do love you!" he snapped. "Why do you think I'm still around?"

"Because you're so far up my father's ass you can't see your own heart," I said. "Now, your adoring public is waiting, and I have work to do. Take care, Jarvis."

I turned on my heel and stalked into the locker room.

I was going to give my father a piece of my mind.

SHERIDAN WENT into labor on Sunday afternoon, and a huge group of us showed up at the hospital to wait for news about the twins. There had been a plan to induce her if she hadn't gone into labor by thirty-six weeks, so she was a week ahead of schedule. Boone and I had been in bed when he'd gotten the call from Wes, so we'd hurriedly showered, dressed, and I'd come straight to the hospital while he'd rushed to Wes and Hadley's to pick up Joey. They'd been kind enough to give us a few hours of alone time, but Hadley wanted to be at the hospital with Sheridan.

"Hey." Hadley looked up as I got to the waiting room.

"Hi." I sank down next to her. "Any news?"

"Not yet."

"Lars must be a mess," I said.

She nodded. "And I think Wes is almost as nervous as he is."

"Your turn is coming soon." I grinned at her.

She rolled her eyes, resting a hand on her stomach. "I can't wait to get him out of me. I'm over being pregnant."

"Soon," I said.

"Is there news?" Sawyer came rushing in, his eyes wide as he looked around.

"Not yet." Nash grinned at him. "We might be here all night."

"Shit." Sawyer took a breath. "You think it'll take that long?"

"Labor is a crapshoot," Hadley said. "When

Annalise was born, Lauren was in labor for sixteen hours. Benny popped out in about thirty minutes."

"Christ." Sawyer sank into a chair and rubbed his hands down his face. "I don't think I have sixteen hours in me."

More friends, teammates, and family members showed up until the waiting room was stuffed to the gills. Some of the guys were pacing the hallway while the rest of us talked and hung out.

I was shocked when my father showed up around five in the afternoon.

"Dad." I got up and greeted him. "What are you doing here?"

He eyed me. "The real question is, what are *you* doing here?"

"Sheridan is my friend," I said, frowning at him. "Where else would I be?"

"Jolie, this isn't your world," Dad said, his voice even gruffer than usual.

"Yes, it is." I met his gaze. "Just because you have to be a hard-ass with the guys doesn't mean I can't be friends with them and their wives."

He scanned the room, obviously looking for someone, and I was glad Boone had opted to hang out at Wes's with Joey and Wes and Hadley's kids. The kids would be far too restless to be here for any length of time, and it was probably better that Boone and I didn't show up together anyway. Our close friends, like Wes and Hadley, knew we were involved, but we'd kept our relationship on the down-low for a plethora of reasons.

"Jolie, I don't know what's going on with you—" Dad began, but he was cut off as another one of the Mavericks, Rory Beauchamp, came into the room.

"Are the twins here yet?" he demanded.

"Not yet," Nash told him.

"Shit." Rory collapsed into the seat between Sawyer and Nash. "I was afraid I'd missed it."

"This is taking too long," Sawyer mumbled. "I'm a wreck."

Suddenly Lars appeared in the doorway, his face tight and drawn. "They are prepping her for surgery," he said in his quiet, accented voice. "One of the babies is in distress."

"Jesus." Nash got up and walked over to him. "Do you need anything?"

Lars shook his head. "No. I just wanted to… update everyone."

I didn't hear what Nash said to him, but Lars's teammates had surrounded him and I tried to tamp down the worry gnawing at my gut. This had to be scary for Sheridan.

I moved away from my dad, pulling out my phone so I could tell Boone what was going on.

JOLIE: Hey. Looks like Sheridan is having a C-section.

BOONE: Shit. I wish I could be there.

JOLIE: Better that you're not. My dad showed up and he's all over me for being here.

BOONE: I'm sorry, beautiful.

JOLIE: Don't worry about me. Just send some good vibes into the ether for Sheridan and the babies.

BOONE: You got it.

JOLIE: I'll see you later, okay?

BOONE: Are you coming over?

JOLIE: You want me to?

BOONE: I'm going to be gone for a week...what do you think?

I smiled as I typed out a response.

JOLIE: I think it's a good thing I didn't wear underwear.

BOONE: You're killing me. You know that, right?

JOLIE: I don't know what you're talking about. LOL

BOONE: See you later, babe.

I stuffed the phone back in my pocket as my father came over to me.

"We should talk," he said.

"Not here, and definitely not now." I shook my head.

"You have to trust me," he said finally. "I know

what's best for you. I've lived this life and it's not all it's cracked up to be. Ask your mother."

"But it was okay when I was marrying Jarvis? Don't be a hypocrite, Dad."

"Guys like Boone will chew you up and spit you out," he said, his voice laced with contempt. "I don't want that for you."

"I'm not talking about this with you in front of the team," I said quietly.

"Then let's go back to the house. Your mother made a pot roast."

"I'm not leaving until the babies are here, but you go ahead."

"Jolie." He stared at me, his jaw working in obvious frustration.

"Dad." I stared right back.

I hated this pissing contest I'd been drawn into, but this was about more than just Boone and me. This was about my life. He couldn't continue to manipulate me like this. It wasn't fair and it was ruining our relationship. Somehow, I had to make him understand that.

The situation was also reinforcing the idea of my leaving St. Louis.

Maybe it was time to set up an interview in New York.

Once Boone was gone, the only thing keeping me

here would be Grandma G, and as long as she was healthy, she and my mother would come visit me wherever I wound up.

As for my father, he was going to have to make a choice.

Either he let go of the control he seemed to need to wield over me, or he wasn't going to be a part of my life anymore.

It was that simple.

CHAPTER TWENTY-ONE

Boone

"Where is she?"

Joey was bouncing in his seat, surveying the parking lot of The Oaks Residential Treatment Center for Emma. I opened my mouth to answer his question, but he spoke again.

"I can't see her," he said. "Where is she, Uncle Boone?"

"She's inside the building, bud. I'm sure if it wasn't so cold, she'd be standing out here waiting for you."

Today was family day at the rehab center. Emma had told me over the phone that she didn't want to break down in front of Joey, but she missed him a lot. I didn't know why, but I was nervous. Joey and Emma needed to see each other, but it was going to be hard for both of them to say goodbye. And what was hard for them would also be hard for me.

I'd always wanted my sister to want more for herself, but now that I knew Joey, there was more at stake. If she chose to go down a bad path again, I wouldn't be able to look away.

"What's my mom doing here?" Joey asked as I parked.

He'd asked me that question no less than twenty-five times, and my answer was the same every time.

"She's working on herself. That's something strong people do."

"My mom is strong. She carries heavy boxes all the time."

I smiled at him in the rearview mirror. "I'm talking about a different kind of strong, Jojo. Strong on the inside."

"Oh."

The Oaks was set on a sprawling, modern campus surrounded by woods. It was a private setting away from the city. My agent Evelyn had found it for me, and she said it was highly rated. Hiking, music, and art therapies were emphasized, though I doubted Emma was doing much hiking in winter.

"How long can we stay?" Joey asked as we walked to the front entrance.

"A couple of hours."

"How many is that?"

I ruffled his hair. "Two, kid."

He clutched his elephant, keeping it close as we went through security and followed the signs for family day. The place was clean and peaceful, with skylights, lots of plants and softly gurgling fountains. A few kids were tossing pennies into a large fountain in an open two-story room where a harp player performed in one corner.

The hallway led us to a room with a few rows of blank canvases set up on easels, small groups of people sitting around tables or standing and talking.

"Joey!"

Emma was rushing toward us, tears shining in her eyes as she approached her son.

"Mom!"

She got down on her knees and he flew into her arms. Emma scrunched her face as she fought tears, and I looked away, a lump in my throat. She held her son for as long as he allowed before pulling away to fire questions at her.

"What do you do here, Mom? Is it hard?"

"Give her a minute," I said. "We'll have plenty of time to talk to her."

When she stood up, I wrapped her in a hug and felt her relax against me.

"I told him I'm going to start charging him a quarter per question," I cracked.

She laughed as she pulled back and looked at me. "Good luck with that."

My sister looked very different than she had the day she arrived at my apartment. Her hair was clean, pulled back in a simple ponytail, and her face was a little fuller. She looked rested, wearing jeans, a gray T-shirt, and tennis shoes.

"Mom, what are those for?" Joey asked, pointing at the canvases.

"Those are for us to paint pictures."

His jaw dropped. "We get to paint on those?"

"Yep. And whatever you paint, I'll hang it up at our new place when I'm done here."

He grinned and looked at me. "Can I paint now?"

A flash of hurt passed over Emma's face, probably because he'd asked me instead of her. I put an arm around her and gave her an encouraging squeeze.

"Whenever your mom wants to," I said.

"Can I, Mom?" Joey begged. "Please?"

"Sure."

We all put on smocks and Emma showed us how to squeeze out paint onto our boards. Joey immediately dove into his painting, looking over at his mom every minute or so to make sure she was still there.

"You paint a lot here?" I asked her.

"Sometimes. It depends on the day. They actually keep us really busy with sessions. I only have about two hours of free time a day. But I have a painting class twice a week, too."

"How's it going? Overall?"

She lowered her brush and looked at me. "It's really good. It's hard, though, you know? Taking a hard look at yourself and seeing where you messed up."

"Yeah. We all do, though."

I'd never heard Emma admit she'd messed up before. Hopefully she was focused on moving forward because getting hung up on past wrongs could lead to a bad spiral. I'd just watched my teammate Sawyer kick his drinking habit, and it was something he admitted struggling with at times.

"How's Andy?" she asked.

"Almost done with his last round of chemo for this treatment. He'll get scans soon to see how it worked."

She nodded, her expression echoing my worries about our brother. "And he's feeling okay?"

"He's hanging in there. He's lost weight. But you know Andy; he's a fighter."

Emma smiled. "I want to take Joey home when I'm done here. I have a lot of amends to make."

I paused, then said, "Are you sure you're ready for that?"

She kept her gaze focused on the canvas, where she was layering on coats of blue and white paint. "It's part of my program. I don't know if Joey and I will stay there, but I need to go there in person to see them."

I nodded, holding my brush in front of the blank canvas in front of me. I hadn't painted in years. What the hell was I supposed to paint a picture of?

"You know you guys can stay with me, right?" I said. "For as long as you need."

She gave me a grateful look. "I'll probably take you up on that."

I looked over both shoulders to make sure no one was within earshot, then spoke in a low tone.

"Just between us, I'm moving home at the end of my season."

Emma's brows shot up. "You mean like a trade?"

"I hope so. But either way, I'm going."

She smiled, looking hopeful. "Then that's where we'll be, too. I hope Mom and Andy will forgive me and we can all spend time together."

Before his cancer diagnosis, Andy was deeply protective of our mom. He resented Emma for her lies and bad treatment of our mom. He was a lot mellower now, though. More focused on what truly mattered.

We painted for around forty-five minutes, Joey whipping out three completed canvases. One of them was a picture of me playing hockey that said, "Mavriks ar the best." It was definitely going to be hung up in my apartment.

"You like it?" I said, flipping my canvas around to show him.

He put a palm to his forehead and laughed. "What is it?"

I furrowed my brow as I glanced down at the face I'd painted, which had tiny eyes, hair going in every direction, and ears that were two different sizes.

"It's you, my dude," I said. "Can't you tell? It looks just like you."

"Uncle Boone, you're one of a kind."

He'd heard that comment from Jolie, and now he repeated it all the time, whether it was relevant or not. She was so good with him, always snuggling with him and reading stories together. She'd always tell him how smart and kind he was. I'd never realized before how important it was to me that my partner be great with kids.

Maybe because I'd never even considered having kids. I wasn't old enough for that yet. Several of my teammates were becoming dads, though, and between that and taking care of Joey, I'd started to think about when I'd be ready.

Lars Jansson was a dad. I still couldn't believe it. My big, awkward teammate had gone from zero to one hundred in the nurturing department since meeting Sheridan. Their babies, Clara and Claudia, had been born the day before yesterday, and he was spamming the Mavericks group text with photos of his kids already.

"You look thoughtful," Emma said as we waited in the buffet line to grab something for lunch.

"I met someone."

She waited for me to say more, but I just shrugged.

"Come on, since when are you shy, Mikey? Tell me about her."

I looked over my shoulders again, irrationally paranoid that Coach would jump out and bust me at the mention of Jolie's name.

"She's my coach's daughter. Jolie."

Joey was in the buffet line between us, and he frowned at the woman who had just scooped food onto his plate.

"Don't be stingy with the mashed potatoes," he said.

Emma's mouth dropped open in shock. "Joey! That is not how we talk to people."

He looked over at me, apparently thinking I was going to bat for him, but I shook my head.

"Can I have more, please?" he asked.

The woman serving the food fought a smile as she added more potatoes to his plate. "How about some gravy, hon?"

"Sure." Emma elbowed him and he added, "Please."

She gave me a look.

"I don't know where he picked that up," I said.

"How are you managing him? With hockey and all?"

"He hangs out with my teammate Wes's wife, Hadley. They've got two kids he loves to play with."

"Benny calls Uncle Boone Uncle Poon," Joey interjected.

"Okay, let's not say that word here," Emma whispered to him.

"What word? Poon?"

I held in my laugh and put a hand on his shoulder. "Yeah, that word. Don't say it again, okay?"

"Okay."

I went back to my conversation with Emma.

"And Jolie takes him places and hangs out with him a lot, too."

Joey looked up at his mom, beaming. "She bought me eight books at the bookstore, and a cookie, and hot chocolate."

"That's so nice, baby. I hope you said thank you."

He nodded. "I did. Jolie says I'm the kindest boy she's ever known."

Tears formed in Emma's eyes and she waved a hand in front of her face. "Okay, so I like her a lot. Are you guys serious?"

I sighed. "We can't be. I'm only here for a couple more months at the most, and she's finishing up school and then getting a job. She's worked hard to get where she is."

"Can't she get a job in Nashville?"

The thought had definitely crossed my mind, but it didn't feel right to ask her that. Jolie had worked every bit as hard toward her career as I had, if not harder, and I didn't want her settling for a job when things were still new with us.

"Are you afraid to ask her?" Emma said.

"Not afraid, just...I don't know. I guess we'll see what happens."

"You seem happy."

I pictured the redhead with legs for days who fueled my fantasies and made me laugh. Yeah, I was happy. But I was also a realist. Things with us depended completely on where she ended up because I had to go to Nashville.

We ate lunch and then Emma and Joey had a session with her counselor. Joey went to a playroom with some other kids after that so Emma and I could have a session together.

She was committed to her recovery. I could see the determination in her face and hear it in her voice. Being a better mom was her goal, and she was laser-focused on it.

"I'm proud of you," I told her when it was time for me and Joey to go. "Keep doing what you're doing."

She wiped a tear from the corner of her eye. "It's been forever since I felt like a person anyone would be proud of. But I'm proud of me, too."

Joey cried and clung to her, begging her to come with us. Her expression was tortured, and I finally had to pry Joey away from her.

"Hey, we have to go, Jojo," I said. "You want to go to that video game place you like so much on the way home?"

He rubbed his eyes with a fist, nodding and sniffling.

"We get to come back and see her soon," I said. "I need you to be strong because she's doing this so she can be the best mom to you."

He nodded, and Emma gave me a grateful look.

"I love you, Joey," she said, holding back tears. "I promise we'll be together again soon, okay?"

"Okay."

I picked him up to carry him to the car, my chest aching as he continued crying.

I understood Lars's pride when it came to his twins and why Wes had given up partying and now spent his free nights watching Pixar movies with his wife and kids.

Joey had done something to me. I loved him in a way I'd never loved anyone before. It was a glimpse of fatherhood, and I felt more ready for it than I'd ever thought I'd be.

CHAPTER TWENTY-TWO

Jolie

With Hadley late in her pregnancy now and Sheridan dealing with newborn twins, I'd been spending more and more time with Joey to give them a break. I didn't mind because he was a great kid. Full of energy, curious about everything, as well-mannered as a four-year-old could be, and he loved all things hockey, which meant I could take him to the rink with me. It annoyed my father to see Joey with me on a regular basis, but he didn't get to camp as often these days, and I'd made sure he understood I was going to help take care of Joey whether he liked it or not. I wasn't sure he was on board, but at least he'd stopped griping about it. I assumed my mother had talked to him.

Either way, I was done being manipulated.

The better news was that Jarvis had started dating a Chicago-based newscaster, and pictures of them were all over the gossip pages online. Dad had been pissed, but that was between him and Jarvis. As far as I was concerned, we'd both moved on.

I certainly had.

Boone was busier than ever as the regular season ended and the team headed into the first round of the playoffs, yet he still found time for me. For us. The lines had begun to blur with whatever this was between us because no matter how casual it was, there was something special there. We hadn't talked about what we were going to do once his season was over and he left St. Louis, but it was hard to imagine my life without him.

He was the whole damn package.

And he liked me just the way I was. Redheaded, nerdy scientist and all.

We talked for hours at night sometimes, especially when he was traveling and I couldn't stare at my laptop screen anymore. He thought my research was fascinating, we enjoyed talking hockey, and we both adored Joey. Not to mention what went on when we were together. I'd never been with a man who knew exactly what I needed. Or one who made me feel as desirable.

His flight had landed a little while ago and he was on his way over. Joey was asleep in my bed, so there wouldn't be any lovemaking tonight, but I'd still put on a sexy, black lace teddy under my yoga pants and long-sleeved T-shirt. The plan was to tease him so he'd be thinking about me until we could be alone together, but in retrospect, this might not have been the best idea.

I couldn't wait for him to touch me. So what the hell did I think was going to happen when I gave him a glimpse of what I'd hidden beneath my clothes?

Well, too late now because he'd just tapped on the door.

"Hi." I opened it with a smile, drinking in how good he looked in slacks and a button-down shirt. Standing there with his shirtsleeves rolled halfway up his forearms, I momentarily forgot that I had a surprise for him.

"Well, hey." He leaned in, his lips finding mine for a soft, lingering kiss.

"Mmm. I've been thinking about that for days." I couldn't help the sigh of pleasure that escaped me.

"Yeah?" He slid an arm around my waist as he nudged me back far enough for him to kick the door shut behind him. "What, exactly, have you been thinking about?"

"The surprise I have for you," I said in what I hoped was a husky voice.

"I like surprises," he said, his blue eyes darkening slightly as he watched me.

"Close your eyes," I said.

He did as I asked and I hurried to the bedroom, peeking in to make sure Joey was still asleep. I softly closed the door behind me and then tugged my top over my head, letting it fall to the ground.

"This is taking a long time," Boone complained.

"It'll be worth it. Patience, Mr. Boone."

"Can I peek?"

"No!" I laughed, pondering whether or not I dared to take off my pants so he could see the full effect. If Joey woke up, I figured I could dart into the bathroom while Boone went to see what he needed, so I made an impromptu decision and quickly wiggled out of my yoga pants.

"Okay," I said softly, turning to face him. "Now you can open your eyes."

"Fuckkkk." He drew the word out for several seconds as he looked me up and down. "What are you trying to do to me, Jolie? That's…" His voice trailed off and he blew out a breath. "That might be the hottest thing I've ever seen."

I ran my hands over my breasts, cupping them lightly as I drew them together. "You like?"

"Do I like?" His voice held disbelief. "I'm so fucking hard I'm about to embarrass myself."

"Now you know how I've felt all week."

"Oh, believe me, I know." He met my gaze. "Now —what are we going to do about it?"

"Unfortunately, with Joey in the bedroom, I'm not sure we have many options." I leaned over and picked up my yoga pants, starting to step into them.

"What do you think you're doing?" Boone demanded, taking three long steps that brought him over to me.

I giggled, playfully peering up at him from under my lashes. "Sorry, big guy, but this was a tease to get you thinking about *next* time."

"Next time?" His eyes narrowed slightly. "Next time is right fucking now." Before I could react, he picked me up and tossed me over his shoulder.

"Boone!" I hissed quietly. "What are you doing? Joey's right in the bedroom."

"You should've thought of that before you put that scrap of nothing on." He moved into the bathroom and shut the door behind us.

My bathroom was tiny, so it wasn't like we'd be able to do anything in here, but Boone seemed to have other ideas.

"Boone, we can't—"

"Yeah, we can." He set me down on the vanity, moving between my legs as he bent his head to kiss me. My mouth opened eagerly and my legs closed around his hips. I wasn't sure what we were doing, but a tornado couldn't have moved me away from him now that he was touching me.

His erection was steely, pressed against my aching core, and I moaned into his mouth as his tongue tangled with mine.

"Boone…" His name left my lips in a breathless whisper as he trailed his mouth along the curve of my shoulder.

"You're so fucking beautiful," he whispered. "Your skin is like silk. I can't get enough of you, Jolie. I want you all the time." His lips skimmed the edge of the lacy fabric, causing goose bumps to break out all over me. He buried his face in my cleavage, lifting my breasts so they rested on top of the underwire that had been holding them. His five-o'clock shadow simultaneously chafed and aroused me, the rough-ness as much of a turn-on as the smoothness of his lips.

Using the tip of his tongue, he traced circles around my areola, teasing and taunting my nipple until it was a hard, taut tip. He nipped with his lips, flicked with his tongue, and suckled with his mouth.

I was beyond aroused, on the brink of detonation. Then he moved to the other breast, starting all over again and leaving me panting with unfulfilled need.

"Boone…"

He clamped down on my nipple, just hard enough to make me whimper, before sucking my breast into his mouth. Pleasure zinged down my spine, landing squarely between my legs, and I dug my fingers into his hair. My head fell back, my chest arching into his face, and he licked and sucked and kissed until I wasn't sure I could take anymore.

"Boone, I need you…fuck me already!"

His mouth was back on mine as he fumbled with his slacks. Then his fingers were between my legs, moving the fabric to the side as he slid into me. We both moaned, and I angled my hips to take him deeper.

"Fuck, that's hot." His hands traveled down to my ass, gripping me tightly as he held me in place. He thrust deep, gliding through my slickness effortlessly.

"So good," I moaned, dragging my nails down his back.

He picked up speed, his body slapping against mine, our lips fusing together.

It was fast and hard and rough.

I wanted to hold out, make it last longer, but my

body was spiraling into a tsunami of lust. Every time he bottomed out, I felt the familiar coiling in my belly, telling me release was imminent.

"Michael!" I grabbed his shoulders, holding on for dear life as my orgasm ripped through me. I did my best to stay quiet, but there was no way to know for sure. I didn't know who or where I was as shock waves of ecstasy rocketed over and through me with enough ferocity to nearly buck me off the vanity.

"Fuck!" Boone's growl told me he was right there with me. He slammed into me one last time, and then there was nothing but a hazy cloud of aftershocks. Each time I shuddered around him, he pressed soft kisses on my cheeks and throat, still holding me tightly, whispering how beautiful and sexy I was.

I wanted to make a joke, say something lighthearted and funny, anything that would ease this intensity that was starting to overwhelm me.

But I was too worked up.

Worked over.

Spent.

I couldn't move, my limbs like jelly as I rested against him.

"You okay?" he asked after a few minutes.

"My body and soul temporarily separated," I

murmured. "Just waiting for everything to come together again."

He chuckled, running his hands up and down my back. "You should wear lingerie more often."

"Okay."

He slowly started to pull out and we both froze as what we'd done seemed to hit us.

"Oh shit, Jolie…I didn't use—" He swallowed as his guilty gaze met mine.

"It's okay," I said quickly, snapping out of my orgasm-induced trance. "I'm on the pill."

"God, I've never done that before. I'm really sorry. We should have talked about it before going without a condom."

"It's fine. Really. I trust you."

And I did.

Every moment we spent together was better than the last. No matter what happened going forward, I had no regrets.

"You sure you're okay?" he asked, his eyes searching my face worriedly.

"Yes." I reached up and put my hands on either side of his face. "I would tell you if I wasn't. Now, you want to take a quick shower?"

"With you?" He circled my waist with his hands. "Absolutely."

I got to my feet and slowly tugged the teddy the rest of the way off.

"You're wearing far too many clothes," I murmured, starting to unbutton his shirt.

"Then undress me."

"What do you think I'm doing?"

"You know I'm going to fuck you again in the shower."

"I was hoping so." I pushed the shirt off his shoulders.

"Does this mean we're done with condoms?"

"Uh-huh." I dropped to my knees, pleased to see him already beginning to get hard again.

"I thought we were taking a shower?"

"We are." I gripped his erection in my hand and slowly pumped up and down a few times. "I just need to do something first."

His head fell back against the wall as he groaned. "Fuck. Yeah."

CHAPTER TWENTY-THREE

Boone

"Do you have any threes?" I asked.

I studied Jolie's face as she considered her hand of cards, Joey giggling from his seat next to her. She bit her lip, which sent a shot of arousal through me, her attempt at a thoughtful expression looking lustful.

Which was becoming a problem. She looked hot fresh out of bed in the morning, wearing sweats at the ice rink, even bundled up in a coat and hat. Every time I looked at her, I wanted to touch her. And since we kept things tame when Joey was awake, I spent a lot of time wanting.

"Go fish," she finally said.

I narrowed my eyes at her and gave Joey a questioning look. "You think I can trust her? I don't know, I think she might be holding out on me."

Jolie dropped her jaw, acting appalled. "Me? I play by the rules, Mr. Boone."

"You can't trust her," Joey said, his eyes sparkling with amusement.

"If you see any threes come out of her hand later, you let me know," I said, running my hand over the pile of cards in the middle of my dining table.

He pointed two fingers at his eyes and then at her, which he'd learned from me doing it to him, and Jolie threw her head back with laughter.

"I think you've got a mini-me," she said.

"What's that?" Joey asked.

She ruffled his hair. "It means you remind me a lot of your uncle."

The doorbell rang and Joey grinned. "Is that the pizza?"

"Probably."

I set my cards down on the table and gave Jolie a warning look. "No cheating while I'm gone."

She scoffed. "I don't have to cheat to beat you. I'm 3–0, fair and square."

When I answered the door, the delivery driver passed me a stack of five boxes, saying, "Thanks for the tip, man. Appreciate it."

I'd tipped him in the app I ordered from, and I nodded as I took the boxes. "Hey, thanks, man. Have a good one."

When I walked into the kitchen, Joey's eyes widened. "That's all for us?"

"Yep. You like cheese, Jolie likes veggie, and I like supreme. And I like leftover pepperoni pizza."

Jolie gave me a look. "So you don't like supreme when it's leftover?"

I cringed. "No. Only pepperoni."

"I'm not sure how to break this to you, but you are kind of high maintenance."

"Ha." I set the boxes on the kitchen island as she pulled three plates out of a kitchen cabinet. "There's nothing more high maintenance than your Starbucks orders."

"Hey, for eight bucks, I'm getting it exactly the way I want it."

"Oh yeah?" I held her gaze from the other side of the island. "And how, exactly, do you want it?"

Joey was oblivious to us, flipping every box open in search of his thin crust with extra cheese.

"I like it with extra pumps," Jolie said, her expression loaded with meaning. "That's the best part for me."

"Uh-huh. Maybe some cream on top?"

She moaned and nodded. "Extra cream, please."

Fuck. Now I was hard, and it was several hours too early for sex. Joey layered three pieces of pizza onto his plate and went into the living room, yelling, "Can we watch a movie now?"

I spoke to Jolie in a low tone, saying, "You're in trouble, young lady."

"Oh, am I?" She gave me a playful grin. "Because I might like that."

I went around the corner of the island, planning to grab her, but she reacted quickly and went around the island, too, keeping herself across from me as I tried to get to her.

Her gaze was filled with challenge. *Chase me, I'm worth it,* she said without even opening her mouth.

She was quick and it took me a little while to catch her, but when I did, I grabbed her around the waist and swept her off her feet against my chest. Both of us were slightly out of breath as we looked at each other in silence for a few seconds.

She was worth chasing and more. Jolie and I clicked in a way I'd never felt with any other woman. Not only did she drive me crazy in the best way, but she was quickly becoming my best friend. She was the one I wanted to talk to when I woke up in the morning and before I went to bed at night. There was no disconnect, which I'd felt with every other woman I'd dated recently. They always wanted more than I wanted to give.

Jolie and I both wanted the same things. Time together. Laughter. Crazy good sex. Friendship. Support. She didn't care about being seen with me because she had a place in the hockey world already from her dad.

"Why did we have to meet now?" I whispered.

Her shoulders dropped. "I know. Right after I ended a big relationship."

"Right before I move to another state."

Neither of us had been looking for love, but it found us anyway. I didn't want Jolie to be any different than she was; I was proud of her hard work and the successful career that awaited her. But it would've been easier if she'd been a puck bunny hoping to follow a man wherever he led.

"I'd still do it," she said, holding my gaze. "Even knowing it can't last, I wouldn't change a thing."

"Me either."

I wrapped my arms around her, pulling her flush against my chest and kissing her. She was even a perfect physical fit—she belonged in my arms.

"You guys, stop kissing!" Joey called from the other room. "Let's watch *The Mighty Ducks*."

I groaned. "Pick something else. We've watched that one three times already."

Joey ran into the kitchen, a half-eaten slice of pizza in hand. "But I love that movie. So does Jolie."

Jolie nodded, a smile playing on her lips. "Why don't we take a vote?"

"Don't bother. I already know I'll lose," I grumbled.

"Yay!" Joey cheered. "Let's go."

I kissed Jolie on the forehead, part of me wishing we could have finished our conversation and part of me glad we were leaving some things unsaid. It wouldn't make things any easier if I told her I was crazy about her. That I thought about what an amazing mother she'd be one day when I saw her with Joey. That I hated when she had to leave, and I'd never felt that for any other woman before.

"Can I get some pizza first?" Jolie asked Joey.

"If you go fast."

I playfully scoffed at him. "How nice of you to let us eat, kid."

"You didn't get the cinnamon bread," he countered.

This kid. He never let anything get by him.

"I forgot about it, dude."

He was standing in front of the fridge, filling the water bottle I'd bought him. That was the only battle I'd won—he mostly drank water now. I'd convinced him that if he kept drinking orange soda, it would turn his teeth orange.

"Okay, I'm ready to watch the greatest hockey movie ever made," Jolie said, her plate piled high with pizza.

I grabbed the box with the supreme in it and carried it to the coffee table, and when I went to sit down, I saw that Jolie was on one end of the couch and Joey was snuggled up to her.

The Mighty Ducks wasn't even a contender for greatest hockey movie ever made, but seeing my nephew so content was worth watching it again. I'd gotten close to him, and it reinforced how little I really knew about Andy's kids.

I wished I could have it all—hockey, my family, and Jolie. But it just wasn't meant to be.

―――――

CLANKING dishes and the smell of freshly brewing coffee woke me up the next morning. I'd fallen asleep on the couch, my neck sore from the awkward position.

"Like that?" Joey asked from the kitchen.

"Perfect," Jolie said. "How did you become such a perfect pancake flipper?"

"Uncle Boone taught me."

I slipped into the bathroom to take a leak and brush my teeth, and when I walked into the kitchen, Joey was tearing into a big stack of pancakes.

"You want some pancakes?" he asked through a mouthful of food.

"I'll make eggs, dude. You eat the pancakes." I approached Jolie and kissed her softly. "Morning. Nice to see you still here."

"Morning. I think we all fell asleep during *Mighty Ducks Two*." She poured a mug full of coffee and passed it to me. "I have to go. I'm going to swing by my place and shower real quick before heading to the lab."

"Can I go with you?" Joey begged.

"Not this time. But I promise I'll take you again soon, okay?"

"Okay."

She gave me a quick kiss and then went over to Joey and kissed the top of his head. "Be good, you two. I'll see you later."

"Bye, babe," I said, walking her to the door.

"Do you love her?" Joey asked when I walked back into the kitchen.

"Whoa, where did that come from?"

He shrugged. "You guys kiss all the time."

"Did she say anything about love?"

He shook his head. "No, but she let me sleep in your bed with her."

"So you two slept in my bed while I was wedged into the corner of the couch? And now I'm stuck with a sore neck?"

"Yep."

I stabbed his top pancake with my fork. "I changed my mind; I'm taking one."

"Hey!"

"You can't eat all those, Jojo. And I'm making eggs and sausage if you want some. But as soon as you finish eating, you need to hit the shower. You're going over to Wes and Hadley's while I go to practice."

Joey groaned. "Are those two babies gonna be there again?"

"The twins?"

"Yeah, they cry all the time."

"That's what babies do. You just have to live with it."

He sighed dramatically. "I don't like babies."

"Less complaining, more eating."

After eating a few bites in silence, he set his fork down. "Uncle Boone, can I be on a hockey team?"

I looked up from the eggs I was whisking. "Hell yeah, you can. I mean, we have to ask your mom, but she'll probably say yes. Andy and I started playing when we were about your age."

"Okay."

Joey was going to be a hockey player. A *great* one. At least if I had anything to say about it.

"So THAT'S what a power play is," I said about an hour later as I turned into Wes and Hadley's neighborhood. "Does that make sense?"

"Yes."

I was about to ask him to explain it back to me when my phone rang through the speakers in my car, my brother's name popping up on the screen. It was unlike him to call in the morning, so I was immediately worried.

"Hey, man, everything okay?" I said in answer.

"Mikey."

His voice was strained with emotion, and my blood ran cold.

No. No, no, no. I wasn't ready. He was going to tell me the cancer had spread, and I wasn't ready to hear it. I'd break down in front of Joey, and that would upset him.

"Hey, can I call you back in ten minutes?" I asked, my throat tightening.

After a moment of silence, he said, "It worked."

I waited for him to elaborate, not breathing.

"I had my appointment this morning, and the chemo worked. There's no detectable cancer left."

He was crying because he was happy. Tears sprang to my eyes and ran down my cheeks.

"It worked?" My voice broke as his words sank in.

"Yeah, I have a couple more tests to clear, but the doctor said I'm probably in remission."

"That's…" I couldn't even think of a word for it.

"I know. Carrie and I haven't stopped crying since we left the doctor's office ten minutes ago. Mom's at church praying because she knew I had this appointment this morning and she doesn't get cell reception there, so she didn't answer when I called her."

"I'm so fucking happy for you, man," I said.

"Thanks. Hey, Mom's calling me on the other line. I have to go."

"Okay, let's talk more later."

"I love you, Mikey."

"Love you, too."

CHAPTER TWENTY-FOUR

Jolie

"Dr. Gizzard, this is excellent work and the committee agrees with me." Dr. Matello peered at me over his glasses, the most recent version of my dissertation in front of him. "I mean it. This is fantastic."

"Th-thank you." I was shocked because technically, I wasn't doctor anyone yet, but the underlying meaning of his words didn't escape me. I'd been expecting another excruciating round of revisions, so the fact that I was done was a wonderful surprise.

"I made a few extremely minor changes—one was nothing but a comma—and you're good to go.

Let's get this baby ready to print and prepare for your defense."

"Are you sure?" My voice was a whisper of disbelief.

"You're ready. I'm ready. It's time. Make sure you invite all the people important to you because your defense day is going to be a big deal for you."

"Then why do I feel like puking?" I muttered, clasping my hands in front of me.

"Ah, we all feel like that." He waved a hand. "Sometimes it's rougher than others, but it's essentially a done deal, Jolie."

"Thank you," I said warmly. "I mean it. I couldn't have done it without you."

"You've been an amazing student, mentee, and friend. You also saved my ass with everything you did for Dr. Camalleri. She was driving me nuts, and when you stepped in to help with the analysis, it freed up my time to do all the other things I need to do."

"I was happy to help," I said, hoping I sounded sincere.

"You're a terrible liar," he said, laughing. "But I appreciate it nonetheless. And a few weeks from now, you're going to be ready to take the science world by storm."

"I don't know about that," I said. "I don't have a job yet, and money is becoming a problem. My parents can't help me forever."

"Speaking of which," he said. "I have news. There's going to be a spot opening up here. Dr. Camalleri is leaving us and I'd like you to take her place."

My mouth fell open. "Really?"

"It doesn't pay a lot, but it's enough to survive and there are benefits like health insurance."

He went on to give me the details, and my head spun with excitement. He was right that it wasn't exactly what I'd been looking for, but I enjoyed teaching and I loved being in the lab. Getting paid to do those things would be a bonus.

Even though it meant staying here in St. Louis when I'd just started getting used to the idea of moving. In fact, I had an interview in New York City with my old professor a few days after my thesis defense.

"I can't give you an answer just yet," I told him since I felt like I owed it to myself to explore some options before committing to anything. I also wanted to be honest with him because he'd been good to me. "I have an interview coming up that I'd like to see through."

"I would have been surprised if you gave me an answer right away," he said, smiling. "Besides, I talked to Joe Kincaid about you just yesterday."

I stared at him. "You know about my interview in New York?"

He chuckled. "Of course. He called to ask me about your dissertation, your work ethic and to get an update on everything you've been doing since you were in his class. Academia is a much smaller world than you think."

"Oh. I didn't realize…" My voice trailed off, wondering if he was upset with me.

"It's a good thing, Jolie," he said gently. "It's one of the reasons I decided to offer you Ellen's position. You're going to have a lot of offers once you get serious about sending out your CV. You're a brilliant scientist who's going to do great things. I can think of a dozen universities that would be lucky to have you on their staff. I hope you decide to stay here, but I'll understand if you find something more exciting." He paused. "That pays more."

We both laughed.

"Why is Ellen leaving?" I asked curiously.

"Her fiancé got a job in California and she's going with him."

"Oh. That surprises me. But good for her."

"It probably happens more than you think. Sometimes we have to make sacrifices for the people we love."

His words gave me pause.

Was I the kind of woman who could follow the man I loved to another city?

Could I leave a job here in St. Louis and follow Boone to Nashville?

Not that he'd asked me to go with him, but I couldn't deny I was in love with him. There was no going back as far as my feelings went, so it was strange that until this moment, I hadn't even considered Nashville an option. He hadn't brought it up either, though, so maybe he wasn't as into me as I was him.

"Jolie?" Dr. Matello was looking at me expectantly and I'd been so lost in thought I hadn't heard what he'd said.

"I'm sorry, what?"

"There are also some new grant opportunities I heard about, if you'd like to discuss the options?"

"Oh. Yes. Absolutely. Thank you."

I put Boone out of my mind and focused on what I needed to do right now.

He'd be gone soon, and my future suddenly looked a lot brighter than it had.

When it was all said and done, I'd worked too hard to give up my dreams for a man.

No matter how I felt about him.

Right?

———

I'D JUST GOTTEN home when my phone rang and Boone's name flashed on the screen. The timing was perfect since I had a lot of exciting news.

"Well, hey there, handsome," I said by way of greeting.

"Hey, babe." His voice sounded funny.

"Are you okay?" I asked cautiously. "You don't sound good."

"No, I'm good." He cleared his throat. "In fact, better than good. My brother got the results of his scans back today."

It took a second for his words to sink in and my breath caught as I realized what that meant. "Oh my god. Does that mean it's...*good* news?"

"Yes. Absolutely."

"Babe..." I didn't even know what to say. This was the best possible news and my eyes filled with tears of happiness. I knew how upsetting this had been for Boone and his whole family.

"They're clear. The scans showed no signs of

cancer, Jolie." He sounded better now, his voice getting clearer as he talked. "It's gone. In remission. Whatever you want to call it."

"Boone!" I squealed with delight. "That's fucking amazing! You must be so happy."

"I can't even put it into words."

I was a little dumbstruck as well.

I was genuinely happy for him and his family, but this changed everything for us too.

If Andy was cancer-free, Boone didn't have to move to Nashville.

Which meant he could stay and, if things continued the way they had been, maybe we could make this work. My father would probably complicate things for us, but we'd figure it out.

"I've been pretty emotional since we hung up," he continued. "Carrie and Andy were both a wreck."

"Of course they were. I don't even know them and I feel a little light-headed."

"I'm still trying to wrap my head around it," he said. "I'm relieved and excited and so many different things, it's hard to put what I'm feeling into words."

"I think that's normal in this situation."

"Not for me. Usually you can't shut me up."

We both chuckled.

"Well, I think we need to celebrate," I said happily. "Because I have good news too."

"Oh yeah? Tell me."

"Not only did Dr. Matello sign off on my dissertation, but he offered me a job."

"Wait, does that mean it's official? You have your PhD?"

"It's not official until my defense day, but yes, I'm essentially done."

"Holy shit, babe, that's incredible! Congratulations."

"It totally caught me off guard. I thought for sure there would be another round of edits."

"And you said there's a job offer too?"

"Yup."

"Here in St. Louis?"

"Yes! So if things go according to plan, I'll be working as a professor and scientist in the near future." I gave him some of the details. "How cool is this?"

"That's wonderful." His voice was quiet. "I'm so proud of you, Jolie. You've worked hard for this and deserve everything you get."

"Thank you."

"Are you still going to interview for the job in New York?"

"I have no plans to take the job, but I think I still need to go, if for no other reason than to gain experience doing interviews, you know?"

"I was just going to say that. And you're going to be an asset no matter where you wind up, so don't shortchange yourself."

"I won't." I took a breath, trying to wrap my head around everything that was happening. "I already looked at the schedule—you're in town the day of my defense. I'd really like you to be there even though it would probably give away our relationship to my dad. But at this point, it doesn't matter as much, does it?"

"No, I guess not," Boone said slowly. "And I want to be there for you. Unless there's a meeting or something I absolutely can't get out of for the team, I'll be there, babe."

"Well, it's on Dad's calendar too, so I can't imagine he'll schedule practice or a meeting in the middle of it."

"Okay. Then count me in."

"Since we have so many things to celebrate, I think we should get naked."

He chuckled. "We'd have to do that right now because Joey is with Hadley, but I have to pick him up by six."

I glanced at the time, 3:55.

"That's not a ton of time for all the things I want to do to you," I teased, "but we can probably make it work."

"Your place or mine?" he asked.

"Your place is closer to Hadley's, which means we'll have a little longer," I said, grabbing my purse. "I'm leaving right now."

I got to Boone's place in record time, throwing myself into his arms the moment he opened the door. Our mouths locked together and he kissed me as tenderly as he did passionately. His fingers tangled in my hair and he held my head, taking his time despite my breathless anticipation.

"You're the most incredible woman I've ever met," he whispered, his mouth close to mine. "I want you to know how proud I am of you. Really."

I smiled. "Thank you. That means a lot."

He kissed me again, his lips a treasure trove of sensual delight.

I loved the way Boone kissed me. Sexy and sweet and delicious.

His hands traveled up my back, skimming beneath my T-shirt until he reached my bra. He unhooked it in one fluid motion and then broke the kiss long enough to pull both the shirt and bra over my head.

"That's what I've been waiting for," he murmured, dipping his head and sucking one nipple into his mouth.

"Me too," I breathed. He would alternate between

biting and kissing, licking and sucking, pulling and nuzzling. It was exquisite torture that I'd recently learned was one of my favorite things.

I was getting addicted to his touch.

Somewhere in the house, his phone rang.

"Do you need to get that?" I asked.

"Nope."

He moved to the other breast, grabbing me by the ass and lifting me up so I could wrap my legs around his waist and my breasts were almost level with his mouth.

His phone started to ring again and he shook his head before I could even ask.

Then my phone started to buzz.

"Boone…" I tugged at his hair. "What if it's Hadley?"

He groaned.

"Talk about a cockblock," he muttered. He set me down and stalked across the room while I dug my phone out of my purse.

It wasn't Hadley who'd called me, but Sheridan, which was odd.

"Hey, man," I heard Boone saying as he came back in the room. "What's going on? Are the twins okay?"

My head snapped up and he nodded, holding up a finger to indicate I should wait.

"What's going on?" I whispered.

"No, of course not. We're on our way. See you in ten!" He disconnected and looked at me. "That was Lars. He and Sheridan are at Wes and Hadley's. Hadley's gone into labor."

CHAPTER TWENTY-FIVE

Boone

"Uncle Poon! My brother is getting borned!" Benny cried as soon as Jolie and I walked through Wes and Hadley's front door.

"I heard, bro." I held out my fist and he bumped it. "Pretty exciting."

"His name is Benny."

I scrunched my face and said, "Really?"

"No," Benny's sister Annalise said, rolling her eyes. "I keep telling you the baby can't be named Benny."

Kon and Lucy came in next, and Benny ran over to them and yelled, "My brother is getting borned! Right now!"

"Nice," Kon said. "You ready to be a big brother?"

"Yeah!"

A baby's shrill wail made us all look upstairs, where the noise was coming from. Lars was descending the open, curved staircase, looking serious as usual.

"I will stay here with the kids," he said. "Sheridan has to nurse nonstop, so we can't leave."

I went back to the family room, where Joey was watching a movie and eating popcorn.

"Hey, man," I said, taking a piece of popcorn and popping it into my mouth.

"Hey. Want to watch a movie?"

"I think Jolie and I are going to the hospital to wait for the baby to be born. Do you want to come with us or stay here?"

"Stay here."

"Okay, I'll pick you up later."

"Let's go!" Nash called as he walked into the room. "Hadley needs me! I'm her birthing coach!"

I laughed at his shit-eating grin.

"Shit, man, that baby won't ever come out if you're the one waiting at the other end of the tunnel."

His girlfriend Sariah laughed as she walked into the room. "Yeah, we're not expecting or anything, but when the time comes, he's only going to be allowed in the room if his mouth is taped shut."

"Good call," I said.

"Come on." Nash put his palms up, looking offended. "A little humor is always a good thing. Lightens the mood."

"Yeah, not when a woman's in labor."

"So we'll take over the waiting room," Nash said. "But we're gonna need to order some pizzas or something. I'm starving." He spotted Joey on the couch and walked over to him, holding out a fist. "What's up, Joey?"

"Hey, Nash."

The foyer got louder as more people came in. Jolie tugged on my sleeve.

"Let's go," she said. "This could happen quickly."

———

"WHAT TIME IS IT?" Rory asked from the other side of the waiting room.

"Time stopped around three this morning," I said.

"It's 5:46," Eric Alvarado said.

We'd been in a private waiting room for twelve hours now, empty pizza boxes stacked on a table and phones plugged into outlets to charge. Some people —like Jolie—were sleeping soundly, but most of us were just sitting here. Jolie was curled up on the love seat we sat on, her head in my lap. I'd needed to piss for the last few hours but hadn't wanted to wake her up.

"You think everything's okay?" Nash said.

Wes was our team captain. He was our leader. Our voice of reassurance. But he wasn't there, and several seconds of silence passed as we all waited to see who would step in for him.

"Everything's okay," Kon said. "Wes told us when he came in a few hours ago that she's just progressing slowly."

"I have a friend whose first delivery took almost twenty-four hours," Lucy said from beside him.

"The first one is usually the longest," Sawyer said. "I'm here no matter how long it takes, so if anyone wants to go home and get some rest, I can text whenever there's any news."

No one said anything, and no one got up. After a few minutes, the door to the waiting room opened and Wes walked in. Everyone sat up straighter, waiting as he ran a hand through his hair.

"Not much to report," he said, his voice weary. "She's exhausted and trying to sleep between the contractions, but it's hard."

"Do you need anything?" Nash asked. "Coffee? Some food?"

Wes shook his head. "No, they're taking good care of us. You think it's going to be like in the movies, where a woman goes into labor and a few minutes later the baby is born, but…"

"Have they said anything about a C-section?" Lucy asked gently.

He nodded. "They said we're not at that point yet, but it's a close possibility. Hadley doesn't want one unless the doctor says she has to have one, though."

When his phone buzzed in his hand with a text, Wes looked at it. "Coach is canceling practice today."

"Thank fuck," I muttered.

"I'm not going on the road trip unless Hadley and the baby are here and doing well," Wes said. "But you fuckers have to go, so go home and get some sleep."

No one moved, and Wes put his hands on his hips, sighing heavily. "Guys"

"We're not leaving," Sawyer said. "Get back in there with your wife and come tell us when to break out the cigars."

Wes nodded, looking at the floor. Two years ago, we had to find a new direction when our team captain, Ben Whitmer, and his wife died unexpectedly. The road was sometimes rocky, but we walked it together as a team.

"Okay." Wes looked around at the faces in the room. "Thanks, guys."

He left the room, and Nash stood up. "Who wants coffee?"

———

IT WAS JUST after nine in the morning when Wes walked into the waiting room, grinning widely.

"Aiden Benjamin Kirby," he said. "Eight pounds, two ounces."

Everyone in the room cheered and got up, crowding around him to hug and congratulate him.

"How's Hadley?" Sawyer asked.

"She's doing great. Completely exhausted, but she was a champ."

Sawyer picked up the box of Cuban cigars he'd brought with him last night. "Whenever you have a chance, let's go outside and light these up."

Wes nodded. "I have to go back down to the nursery where they've got Aiden and then make sure Hadley's good."

"Take your time," Sawyer said.

"Wait, he's in there right now?" Nash said. "We can see him through the window?"

"Yeah, come see him," Wes said. "I don't mean to be a dick, but we're only having immediate family around him and Hadley for now."

"We get it," Eric said. "You guys don't want your newborn around a bunch of germs."

Nash hustled toward the door. "Aiden needs to meet his Uncle Nash first."

Everyone hurried to follow, a crowd of us bursting into the hallway all at once. Jolie slipped her hand into mine and I gave hers a little squeeze as we made our way to the other end of the floor, where the nursery was.

"Oh, look at the babies," Sariah said. "I swear I just felt a pang directly in my ovaries."

"How can you not?" Jolie said, her tone dreamy.

"There he is," Wes said proudly, pointing to a back corner of the room.

A nurse saw us and held Aiden up so we could get a look at him. He was wrapped up in a blue blanket, a little white cap on his head.

"Wes, he's perfect," Sawyer said.

I walked over and put my arm around Wes, emotion welling in my throat.

"He'd be so proud of you," I said.

Wes put a hand over his eyes to cover his tears, his shoulders shaking as he cried. Sawyer came over and put an arm around him from the other side. There was no filling the hole Ben had left in our lives, but we'd never forget him. Wes and Hadley were raising Ben and Lauren's kids as their own, which just showed how strong the bond between teammates could be.

The team was a second family to me, but being here reminded me that I missed these occasions when they happened in my actual family. Hockey had kept me from being there for the births of Andy's kids.

Andy's illness had been the catalyst for me to move back home. And even though he was in remission, I still needed to go. I didn't want to miss every birthday and youth hockey game anymore.

Jolie smiled warmly at me and I felt a physical pain in my chest. It was so damn unfair how this was going down. She'd gotten a great job offer right here in St. Louis, and I knew she thought that since Andy was in remission, I wouldn't be going to Nashville.

I needed to go, though. Much as it hurt, it was the right choice. And even though things were still new with us, I selfishly wanted to ask her to move with me.

What kind of asshole asked that of a woman who was about to finish her doctorate after years of hard work? Her family was here, and she loved them just as much as I loved mine.

Everyone got out their phones to snap pictures of Aiden as the nurse rolled him back toward Hadley's room on a little cart with a clear dome on top. Wes followed along beside her, looking prouder than any hockey trophy could ever make him.

I wanted this. A family of my own. And Jolie was the perfect partner. Things had just started with us, but I felt it deep down. She was a total package, and she made me a better version of myself.

"Who wants to go get some breakfast?" Nash asked after we said goodbye to Wes. "I'm about to waste away over here."

"Want to?" I asked Jolie.

"I wish I could, but I need to shower and get to the lab."

She'd stayed all night, even when I'd told her to take my car home and get some rest. Jolie was everything I'd ever wanted in a woman and more.

"I'll drive you," I said, kissing her.

"No, go have breakfast. I can take an Uber."

"I'm driving you. I need to go get Joey anyway, and I'll take him out for breakfast."

She nodded and smiled up at me. "Thanks."

"Thanks for being here."

"I wouldn't have missed it." She hesitated, then said, "I hope to be with you at lots of occasions like this in the future. I hope that's not presumptuous of me."

I smiled at her, though it wasn't sincere. I couldn't lie and pretend I planned to stay here. It was written all over her face; she wanted me to tell her I wanted the same thing.

And I did, but it was impossible. We couldn't live in two different states and have the relationship we did now.

"You guys coming?" Nash asked, saving me from having to respond to her.

"Nah, I need to go get Joey."

"Okay, I'll catch you later. You too, Jolie."

"Bye, Nash."

I held on to her hand as we left the hospital, not letting on what I was thinking. That soon, I'd have to let go forever.

CHAPTER TWENTY-SIX

Jolie

GRANDMA G HAD BEEN ASKING about Joey, so I brought him over to my parents' house on Sunday while the team had practice. Dad was obviously at practice too, and my mother was out to brunch with friends, so I figured Joey and Grandma could watch *The Mighty Ducks* together while I got a little work done on my laptop. Then I was considering introducing Grandma to Boone. She'd asked at least fifty times, and I knew they'd get along.

"Granny G, Goldberg is the bestest goalie ever!" Joey announced, referencing the movie.

Grandma G pretended to consider it. "Well, maybe. But I'm a big fan of Konstantin Volkov."

Now Joey was pondering. "He's pretty good too. But Goldberg has magic."

"Does he? What kind of magic?"

"The hockey kind."

I stifled my laughter, thinking how much I loved this kid. I was so glad Boone didn't have to leave now. Although that didn't necessarily mean his sister and Joey would settle here in St. Louis, at least I'd still have access to him through Boone. If they all moved to Nashville, chances were we'd never see each other again.

And that was unfathomable at this point.

The movie ended and I started gathering Joey's things. He seemed to make a mess no matter where he went or what we did, and it was second nature now to pick up after him. He had a set of toys that stayed at my apartment now because he was there so often, and Grandma G got him a present every time she saw him.

I hoped my parents would get on board eventually too.

Once they realized Boone and I were serious, Dad would get over it. He had to. And Mom already suspected, but she wouldn't rat me out. Not until we were ready to come clean. Grandma G was totally on board, and Dad always had a hard time going against his mother.

Jarvis was still dating that news anchor or whatever she was, so Dad couldn't very well keep pushing him to work things out with me anymore either.

Well, my father was nothing if not persistent, but that felt wrong even for him.

Eventually, he had to see reason and understand that I wasn't going to let him dictate my personal life. I wasn't a child. Hell, I'd just become a scientist with a PhD. I had a job offer and a lot going for me. He had to get past this need to control his little girl.

I'd just gotten Joey's shoes on when I heard a noise in the kitchen, and my grandmother and I both started.

My mother never came in through the kitchen and their housekeeper didn't come on Sundays.

Which meant Dad was home.

Shit!

"Jolie?" Dad called to me and I cringed. Grandma G got up and took Joey's hand as if that would somehow protect him. Not that Dad would do anything to hurt him, but his growl tended to intimidate two-hundred-pound hockey players, so he'd undoubtedly freak Joey out if he went on one of his rants.

"In here, Dad."

"Hey. What are you—" He cut off abruptly when he spotted Joey. "What the fu—"

"Malcolm!" Grandma G spoke his name sharply, cutting him off before he got the f-word out.

"We were just leaving," I said quickly. "Boone was at practice and Hadley just had a baby, so I've been helping out, Dad. That's all. I'm taking him home now."

Dad grunted, still eyeing Joey like he was the Antichrist coming for a personal visit.

"Hi! I'm Joey!" Joey had no idea what was going on and he broke free from Grandma G, running over with an extended hand. Just like Boone had taught him. I would have been so damn proud if it were literally anyone else.

Dad seemed startled at first but then reluctantly extended his hand. "I'm Coach G."

"Granny G and Coach G! Is she your mommy?"

Dad frowned, his face momentarily softening. "Yeah."

"Cool beans!" Joey raced back over to me, bouncing on the tips of his toes. "Is this your daddy, Jolie?"

"Yup." I couldn't exactly deny it.

But Joey had the attention span of a gnat. "Are we going to get pizza now? Pretty please with sugar and icing on top?"

I managed a tight smile. "I don't know what Uncle Boone has planned, but we'll see."

"Jolie, can I see you in the kitchen?" Dad asked.

I sighed. "Okay. I'll be right back. You guys can go get in the car." I gave Grandma G a look, telling her to get him out of the house. Just in case there was yelling.

"Dad, this isn't the time," I said once we were in the kitchen.

"When is the time, Jolie? I warned you and I sure as fuck warned him."

"Why are you warning two legal, consenting adults about whom they can spend time with?" I demanded. "Seriously, Dad. Enough is enough. Did you think I was still a virgin? Did you think the dirty, filthy things adults do behind closed doors didn't happen with your precious Jarvis?"

"That's not necessary!" he snapped.

"But it is. Because you've made it necessary. I don't need or appreciate you telling me who I can date. So what if he's on the team? He's nice to me. Nicer than Jarvis ever was. Ever." I emphasized the last word.

"He's nice because he's using you!" Dad said, throwing up his hands. "He wasn't going to get in your pants by being a jerk. But that's not real. Don't you know what these guys are like? How they treat women? You think there's such a high divorce rate among professional athletes because they're faithful?"

"But Jarvis was going to be faithful?" I countered. "How come Jarvis got to break all your rules and everyone else is just terrible?"

"Because I could control him! Because he knew what would happen if he hurt you."

"But he did hurt me," I said quietly. "And the only thing that's happened as a consequence is you persistently trying to get me to forgive him."

That telltale vein on Dad's forehead was starting to throb and we stared at each other in a veritable standoff. "So are you going to Nashville with him then?" he asked finally.

"What?" I shook my head. "The situation has changed. He's not going anywhere."

He stared at me. "Jolie, we literally just talked about it not thirty minutes ago. As soon as the season is over, he's being traded. Nashville didn't make the playoffs, so we've made some discreet inquiries. It's going to happen as soon as we can legally do it."

I frowned, a sharp pain shooting through my gut. "I don't believe you."

He shrugged. "Then I guess you need to ask him."

"I will." I turned on my heel and stormed out of the house.

————

PRACTICE HAD ENDED EARLY, so I texted Boone and told him where we were going. I'd promised Joey and Grandma G lunch, and I figured Boone and I could talk while Grandma kept Joey busy.

I was more furious with myself than I was with Boone because he'd never actually said he was staying in St. Louis.

I'd made an assumption and we all knew how that usually went.

"You okay?" Grandma G asked quietly once we were sitting down.

"I don't know," I muttered, handing Joey the crayons the waitress had brought over.

"Talk to him," she whispered. "Tell him how you feel."

It was probably a bad idea to have Boone come meet us, but the day's plan had already been set in motion and I felt helpless to stop this freight train that had begun to roll over my life.

"Hey, guys." Boone walked over to the table with a smile. He scooped Joey up since he'd run to meet him but immediately held out his hand to Grandma G. "You must be Marjorie. Michael Boone."

"Well, hello." Grandma G grinned as she shook

his hand. "It's so nice to officially meet you, although I feel like I know you from watching all the games."

"You a hockey fan?"

"Is that even a question?" she asked, shaking her head. "I raised a hockey player, you know."

Dad had played until a knee injury forced him into retirement.

"Forgive me." Boone chuckled.

Boone leaned over to brush his lips across mine. "Hi."

"Hi." I couldn't look at him and forced myself to concentrate on the menu even though I wasn't hungry anymore.

"Granny bought me a train!" Joey said excitedly. "But Jolie wouldn't let me bring it in the rest-rant."

"Rest-aur-ant," Boone said, enunciating carefully.

"Rest-er-ant." Joey repeated, making us all chuckle.

"You can show me the train later. Thank you," he said to Grandma G. "You don't have to buy him things."

"Ah, I like seeing him smile," she responded.

We ordered and I picked at a Cobb salad while Joey talked nonstop about everything we'd done today.

"Everything okay?" Boone asked at one point, his

voice low as he reached under the table to gently squeeze my thigh.

"I don't know," I admitted.

He frowned, but there was no way for us to talk now, leaving me more and more agitated.

"I have to go potty," Joey said.

"I'll take him." Grandma G was out of her chair faster than I'd seen her move in years.

"Oh, you don't have to—" Boone began, starting to get up.

"But I have to go too." Grandma G shrugged. "It's no problem. Finish eating." She took Joey's hand and they moved away from the table.

"That doesn't feel like a setup at all," he said dryly. "What's going on?"

I took a breath. "Dad came home earlier than anticipated."

"Oh shit. Was he pissed about Joey?"

"Yeah. But then I tried to reason with him, make him understand that me dating you is no different —in the grand scheme of me dating a hockey player—than me dating Jarvis. I called him a hypocrite."

"Okay." There was a weird look on his face as if he knew what was coming, and dread filled me.

"And then he asked me if I was going to Nashville with you."

Neither of us spoke for several long, deadly quiet seconds.

"Jolie—" he began.

"You're still going?" I interrupted in confusion. "Even now that Andy is okay?"

"Well…yeah. I told you that from the beginning. You know how I feel about being close to my family after everything that's happened. And once Em gets out of rehab, she's going to need all of us more than ever. Joey needs all of us too."

"But…" I couldn't finish my thought. I realized what this meant.

He didn't love me.

He didn't want me to go with him.

This had been nothing but a fling to him.

"I'm sorry," he said. "You're…amazing. Beautiful and smart and—"

"Stop!" I hissed under my breath. "Don't do that whole it's-not-you-it's-me song and dance."

"It's not—" He tried again, but I held up a hand.

"I said stop. For fuck's sake, don't patronize me." I got up, yanking my keys out of my pocket and holding them out to him. "Go get Joey's car seat out of my Jeep."

"But—"

"Could you just do what I'm asking before Grandma and Joey get back?"

"Can I finish a sentence?"

"No." I stared at him, my jaw working in frustration.

"Jolie." He reached for me but I took a step back.

"Get the seat out of my car. Then come back in here, say your goodbyes to Grandma, take Joey, and go home. Can you do that?"

"Is that what you want?"

"Yes."

We stared at each other again, the look in his eyes inscrutable as I waited for him to do as I asked.

"Okay." He slowly took the proffered keys and walked out toward the parking lot.

I sank back into my chair, trying to still my shaking hands.

This hurt much more than I'd been expecting, so the sooner I got away from him, the better it would be.

I hadn't cried a single tear over Jarvis, but there would be many, many tears for Boone.

CHAPTER TWENTY-SEVEN

Boone

Mavericks Group Text

Lars: *I finally got a photo of both girls with their eyes open where neither one of them is crying.*

Kon: *Cute.*

Drew: *You've sent us more pictures of your daughters than I have of my kids from their first year.*

Lars: *I can't help how photogenic they are.*

Wes: *Here's Aiden milk-drunk...*

Nash: *That's the same face you make when you're drunk. But seriously, the kid looks like you.*

Wes: Future lady killer. I made sure the doctor was careful when she had that scalpel near the family jewels.

Rory: How'd you manage that?

Wes: I glared at her through the window the whole time.

Lars: Here are the girls in their Mavericks outfits.

Lars: And a few from their first bath...

Drew: You're never going to stop, are you?

Lars: No.

I TAPPED my stick against each of my shin guards three times, then dropped my stick to the concrete floor and practiced puck handling without a puck.

This was part of my ritual. On game days, there were things I always did the same way. Hell, nearly every guy on my team had rituals, whether they admitted it or not.

I'd missed my pregame nap, spending the whole hour staring at the ceiling and wondering how I'd fucked things up so badly with Jolie.

Of course I was planning to tell her about Nashville. We'd just never gotten any time alone for me to do it, and then she'd blown up at me after Coach told her, which he shouldn't have done. He was at the top of my shit list now, and I'd been avoiding him all day.

I'd eaten my pregame meal—a sub sandwich from my favorite deli and an unsweet iced tea—alone in the weight room. I wasn't in the mood to look at one of Lars's three hundred baby photos. There was no one but Jolie I wanted to talk to right now, but she wasn't responding to my texts.

I went into the locker room and put on my headphones, turning on my pregame playlist. My head wasn't where it needed to be for this game. Going to Nashville was the right move, but it wasn't an easy one.

Not only was I losing Jolie, I was also going to lose my teammates. I couldn't imagine calling another team my own. I'd have to, though. It was possible I'd be a fucking mess with a new team, too. I was used to Wes and Nash. I knew how they moved and could anticipate their choices.

A tap on my shoulder made me look. With my elbows resting on my knees, I could see Nash standing there, grinning at me.

"What?" I said, turning off the music.

"Who pissed in your cornflakes?"

I sat up straight, glaring at him. "What do you want?"

He turned his phone screen toward me. "Just wanted to show you this."

It was a photo of Joey, grinning in a Mavericks

hoodie while standing with the team mascot, Ricky the Raven, on the red carpet that had been put on the ice for the national anthem singer. He was clearly excited, giving a thumbs-up for the picture.

"Tell Sariah I said thanks," I told Nash. "I owe her a trip to that salon she likes."

With my usual three babysitters—Hadley, Sheridan, and Jolie—all out of commission, Sariah had offered to keep Joey today and tonight for the game. She worked in the Mavericks front office, so she'd brought him to the arena and he'd be seeing his first professional game tonight.

"She's happy to do it," Nash said. "Just don't be surprised when he comes back wanting to listen to nothing but Taylor Swift."

I couldn't even force a smile. All I could think about was how much I wanted to walk into Coach Gizzard's office and punch him in the face. He'd sabotaged things for me and Jolie, and not only was it unprofessional, but it meant he was a bigger dick than I'd realized before.

Someday I'd be able to tell him to kiss my ass. Someday soon, now that I'd been unofficially told I was getting my trade. I couldn't wait to flip Gizzard the bird on my way out of here.

"What's going on with you, man?" Nash asked, sitting down next to me.

He was my friend, but it was all I could do not to tell him to fuck off. I wanted to be alone with my misery.

"Nothing I want to talk about," I said.

"So a certain redhead, then."

I exhaled heavily, letting my head fall back to rest against the side of my locker. "Do you know what it means when someone says they don't want to talk about something?"

"Yeah, I just don't believe you."

I narrowed my eyes. "Well, even if I wanted to talk about it, which I don't, this isn't the place."

Nash lowered his voice. "Because of *Izzardgay?*"

"Why are you such a fucking idiot? Everyone knows pig latin."

"Just keeping the mood light, bro."

My mood was about as light as a fucking tank, and I wanted to get back to the Eminem song I'd been listening to.

"So she dumped you," Nash said.

Instead of responding, I put my headphones back on, pushed play on my playlist, and closed my eyes. It would be a hell of a long time before I wanted to talk to anyone about things with Jolie. Unless it was Jolie herself, who had to stop freezing me out at some point.

Hopefully.

———

"LOOK AT YOUR LITTLE MUSTACHE, Mikey boy. Did your balls finally drop?"

We were playing Vancouver, and Craig Masterson was the mouthiest dick on his team. He actually might have been the mouthiest dick in the entire league, come to think of it.

"You're supposed to score, did anyone tell you that?" I said, deliberately bumping into him as we waited for play to resume. "You remember what it feels like to score?"

Masterson was on a major skid, and my shot had been a direct hit. He scowled at me and I grinned, determined to make him throw the first punch.

"That big net down there is where you're supposed to put the puck," I said. "You use that stick in your hand."

"Eat shit, Boone," he muttered. "You're the fucking weak link in your line, and everyone knows it."

His shot landed like a physical blow. It was true—Wes and Nash were both better players than me. But this wasn't the right day to point it out, and Masterson sure as shit wasn't the one to be doing it.

"You're a has-been, man," I said, skating over slowly to get in his face. "Time to take your arthritic knees to the nursing home and watch hockey on TV while you eat your pudding."

"You want to fucking go?" he asked, his face reddening.

"Yeah, man, show me how the old folks throw down. Beat me with your fucking cane. You're an embarrassment to this game, still playing at your age."

Masterson tossed his gloves off and drove a punch into my stomach. I felt a brief pang of guilt as I threw my own gloves down. Joey's first hockey game and his uncle gets into a fight.

Then again…he'd probably think it was cool. And this was part of the game. When I was in a shit mood, it was my favorite part.

Masterson shoved me into the boards and hit me again. I deserved it. But he did, too. Both of us had been dicks and we'd both end up with penalties. I needed to get as many hits in as I could. My fists flew and I felt a trickle of blood fall from my nose. Then the refs and our teammates descended on us, the ref trying in vain to pull us apart.

It took Lars, the strongest guy on our team, to get me off of Masterson.

"Fuck you, Boone!" he yelled, pointing at me as two of his teammates held him back by the chest. "You're a fucking asshole."

"Means a lot, coming from you!" I yelled. "Knit me some booties when you get to the nursing home!"

"Boone, enough," Lars said. "Go cool down in the box."

Two minutes wasn't nearly enough, though. I was more fired up than ever when I skated back onto the ice after my penalty, but lines were changing and I had to go to the bench.

Wes glanced over at me and said, "You okay?"

"Yeah, I'm good."

"Keep it together. We need this one."

"Yeah, I will."

Somehow, I managed to keep my focus on hockey for the rest of the game, which we won 3–2 in overtime. Even scoring the winning goal didn't make me feel much better.

Coach and I continued avoiding each other after the game. I checked my phone before hitting the shower and was disappointed to not find a text from Jolie.

Had she watched the game? She usually did. And when she did, I had a congratulations text waiting.

I stared at the screen for a few seconds, wanting to text her. What would it accomplish, though? I'd texted her at least a dozen times since she'd made me leave the restaurant the other day.

The adages about redheads appeared to be true. Jolie was the only redhead I'd ever been with, and now I knew that when she was pissed off, it was a watch-out-world situation.

"Don't do it," Nash said from nearby. "She'll text you eventually. Give her some space."

Space. What the hell did that even mean? When two people were right for each other—and Jolie and I were—they didn't need space. They needed to be face to face, talking out their problems or yelling them out if needed.

Walking away was never the answer. Not when you were all in. I'd walked away from women before because I wanted to avoid making the end any harder than it had to be.

This wasn't the end for me and Jolie, though. It couldn't be. We could date long distance if we had to. I wasn't ready to give up on us, and I didn't think she was, either.

Nash had the worst track record with women before he started dating Sariah. So whatever he said, the opposite was probably the thing to do. Not that I had a choice. I couldn't wait for Jolie to cool down. There was nothing cool about our relationship, and I liked it that way.

I pushed her contact on my phone and typed out a message.

Boone: We need to talk. You can yell and throw things if you want, but we're talking.

The three little dots that indicated she was writing back popped up on the screen, and my heart raced hopefully.

I waited, willing her message to appear on my screen. The dots disappeared, though, and after two full minutes of staring at my phone, I realized she wasn't going to respond.

Fuck. I couldn't take much more of this.

CHAPTER TWENTY-EIGHT

Jolie

HOCKEY CAMP WAS DONE for the season, but with nothing else to do tonight, I went up there anyway. It was quiet at dinnertime. Since camp had the place reserved all winter, there were no men's league games scheduled until nine or ten, and it was both eerie and comforting to have the place all to myself. Not entirely, of course. Gil was somewhere in the back, probably sharpening the rental skates. There was a maintenance guy any time they were open and someone was up front answering the phone and puttering on the computer.

Out here, though, I was alone.

I had my skates but didn't feel like skating.

Mostly I wanted to think.

Maybe brood a little.

Boone had reached out repeatedly, and I hadn't responded because I was hurt and furious, but it was more than that. I was sad and frustrated and…much as I hated to admit it, lonely. And loneliness wasn't a good reason to get back together with a man. I had to sort out my own shit first.

Grandma G was the only person I could count on in my life regularly. I had my parents, of course, but they weren't part of my daily life anymore. If there was an emergency, they'd be there in an instant. Mom and I would occasionally go shopping or meet for lunch, and sometimes she'd call to tell me the latest scrape my cousin Byron had gotten into.

Beyond that, I was an adult and she and my dad had their own busy lives.

I had friends and coworkers at the university, but that was different. We didn't have the text-all-day-and-meet-up-for-something type of relationship.

Real friends, the kind you turned to when your boyfriend broke your heart, hadn't been part of my life for a long time. I could blame it on my studies. That was easy because it had kept me busy. Much busier than people probably thought, but it wasn't like I couldn't have made time for friends. I'd simply chosen not to.

Then I'd met Boone. And Hadley and Sheridan and Sariah and…I sighed as my phone buzzed and Sheridan's name popped up in our group text. We'd started one while we'd all needed to keep in contact to coordinate Joey's schedule, but it had turned into genuine friendship. Something I hadn't had before as an adult.

Sheridan: You guys…if you ever let on you've seen this video, or show it to the guys, I'll kill you, but is my man the hottest, sweetest, sexiest daddy on earth or what?!

I couldn't resist clicking on the video and sure enough, Lars had a twin in each of his arms. He was walking around the nursery singing a Swedish lullaby to them. His voice was deep and soft and surprisingly on key, and I was momentarily mesmerized. Sheridan had probably been, too, as she'd stood there recording.

Oh yeah. Lars represented everything any woman could ever want in a life partner.

All the things I wanted someday.

With Boone.

Tears filled my eyes and I swiped at them angrily, annoyed with myself for still being so broken up about this.

Trying to think about something else, I typed a reply.

Jolie: Did your ovaries explode? Are you already preg-

nant again?

Hadley: Bite your tongue! Wait until you go through childbirth. You wouldn't ask a question like that.

Sariah: I was going to ask the same thing. LOL

Jolie: See?

Sheridan: My ovaries did explode. And yes, we're going to try to get pregnant again. Just not today. Or tomorrow.

Hadley: I'm guessing next week isn't looking good either?

They continued with their banter, but I put the phone down, staring at the ice.

I didn't know what to do and I couldn't talk to the girls about my situation for so many reasons. The biggest was respecting Boone's privacy, and there was no way to explain the breakup without telling them everything. Then, once he was gone, I wouldn't be dating a guy on the team anymore and I'd undoubtedly be busy with my new job. Eventually, our current bond would fade into polite hellos and maybe a wave if I got to the occasional game.

I rubbed my eyes and then rested my forearms on my thighs.

It was odd not having anywhere to go or anything specific to do. The last few months had been a wild ride, between working at hockey camp, finishing my dissertation, helping with Joey, spending time with my Mavericks family, and of course, falling in love with Boone. My life had been full. Rich. Meaningful. And if I was honest, the best parts had nothing to do with my work in microbiology.

I'd always assumed that my work, getting my PhD and eventually a job in my field would consume me into my mid-to-late thirties. That it would fulfill me until I was ready for a baby or two. And until Boone, the man I would have those babies with, had never had a face or a name or even an essence. He'd been some sort of existential figment of my imagination who would father my children. Love hadn't played even the smallest role in that equation. Especially not when I'd been with Jarvis.

Now everything was different.

I was different.

My work was still important, but it wasn't *everything*. Hell, right now it barely registered on my radar, despite being so close to reaching my goal.

And I had to think about why.

I also had to think about who.

Not just Boone, but the friendships I now had, and more than anything else, finding balance going forward. All work and no play had left me emotionally bankrupt. It had me rethinking a lot of the things I thought I knew.

And it was time to figure it out.

———

I SPENT a restless night tossing and turning, so I groaned when my phone rang at eight thirty in the morning.

Grandma G.

I momentarily panicked but then remembered she'd been great about checking in. She was the only person who knew what was going on, but she'd always been there for me and this was no different.

"Hi, Grandma." I tried not to yawn in her ear.

"How are you, sweetie?"

"I'm okay."

"You know you're a terrible liar."

I chuckled. "I'm as okay as someone with a broken heart can be."

"Have you talked to him?"

"No. I've been doing some soul-searching."

"And?"

"Some things have to change once I finish with my PhD. I love my work, but it can't be the *only* thing."

"Thank god," she muttered. "Been hoping you'd figure that out for years."

"Sorry. I guess I'm slow sometimes."

"Have you had any epiphanies?"

"All I know for sure is that I need friends and family and all the things I somehow deprived myself of all these years while I've been in school. But I'm not ready to talk about it yet."

"Are you ready to talk to Boone?"

"What's there to say?"

"How about some of what you just told me?" She paused. "Did it ever occur to you that he was going to ask you to go with him?"

"I don't think he was."

"How do you know?"

"I don't know for sure, but he had months to bring it up. He never did."

"You're about to get your doctorate. You have a job offer here in St. Louis and an important interview in New York City. If he cares about you at all, he wouldn't just assume you'd be willing to give all of that up for him."

I sighed, swinging my legs over the side of the bed and getting up to pad into the kitchen.

I needed coffee before we could have the rest of this conversation.

"I just got up, Grandma," I said, holding the phone between my shoulder and ear as I put water in the coffee maker. "Can we do this later?"

"Nope." She sounded annoyingly chipper and

pleased with herself. "I gave you a little time to come to your senses, but you and Boone are both stubborn, so now I'm stepping in. Call him."

"And say what?"

"How about something like, hey, dickhead—what's your deal? Did it ever occur to you I might want to come with you and get a job at Vanderbilt? By the way, do you love me or not?"

I was so startled at her use of the word dickhead, the phone popped out from where I'd had it wedged, nearly landing in the sink as I flailed to catch it. "Jesus, Grandma, you know I just got up," I muttered, stifling a laugh.

"What, you think I spent my life in hockey arenas and never heard the word dickhead?"

"No, but I've never heard you use it."

"It isn't usually appropriate. In this context, it is."

I adored this woman.

I'd won the fucking grandparent lottery with her.

"I don't know what to say or do," I admitted. "Because even if he did ask me to go with him, I don't have a job in Nashville. Yes, Vanderbilt is there and potentially an option, but we don't know that they have openings, much less whether or not they'd want me."

"There are labs and such there, too," she said. "And frankly, you're both young. Things can change, no matter what the current plan is. Maybe he'll get an offer that's too good to refuse. Twenty million for one year in Vancouver."

"Grandma—" I started to protest.

"I *know* it's not feasible," she said, snickering as if she'd amused herself. "I'm exaggerating about that, but I'm not exaggerating about the fact that life happens. For all he knows, his brother could get the same offer in Tokyo. Or his sister might meet a man and move to Arkansas. While his parents decide to retire to Florida. Right now, the plan is Nashville. Great. In five years, it could all change. Trust me on this. Life has a way of throwing curveballs."

"I understand the point you're making, but it actually makes it worse for me, not better."

"Why? Because if you get a job and five years' worth of experience under your belt at Vanderbilt, the people at UCLA wouldn't want you? Your PhD isn't linked to one city or state. Would you stop making excuses. Do you love him or not?"

"It's not that simple."

"Oh, but it is. Answer the question, but answer it thoughtfully, using both your heart and your brain. Take a minute."

Did I love him?

Enough to move to Nashville and then to

Vancouver or Tokyo or wherever life took us, no matter what it did to my career?

I didn't have to think that hard.

I did love him that much.

I loved him more than anything.

And just because I was comfortable here, and I'd probably get comfortable wherever I landed next, the truth was I could be a scientist almost anywhere.

The lab experience I'd gotten during grad school and the papers I'd already published left me in a good position professionally. Nothing was guaranteed in life, but that was the whole point. Life could and most likely would throw me a lot of unexpected options, and the one thing that needed to be constant was the people in my life.

No matter where I went.

I could foster long-distance relationships if I made them a priority.

Friendships didn't have to end because the current situation did.

And the same thing applied to Boone.

If he loved me, and that was still a big if, we could make it work.

No matter what else happened, he was the one I pictured myself getting through the bad times with.

Laughing with at breakfast every morning.

Working with to make a life together.

Having children with.

Loving for the rest of my life.

That was the only question now.

We'd never used the *L* word, though I'd felt it a few times. If I was honest, I'd held back emotionally because this was supposed to have been casual. If he'd been thinking the same thing, maybe he was as reluctant to put his heart on the line as I was. We both needed to be more open and honest, no matter what that looked like. He might still break my heart, but since we'd never talked about anything long term, I had no way of knowing what he was feeling.

And there was only one way for me to find out.

Grandma and I finished our conversation and I promised her I would think about everything she'd said, and then finally took my first sip of coffee.

I closed my eyes as the strong brew worked its way into my system.

It was time.

I had to reach out and find out whether I had a future with Boone.

My fingers shook a little as I typed out a text because I wasn't quite brave enough to hear his voice yet.

Jolie: Hey. I know you're busy with the playoffs, but if you'd still like to talk, I'm home. Or I can meet you somewhere. Let me know.

CHAPTER TWENTY-NINE

Boone

"I'M READY! Is it time to go yet?"

Joey was bouncing off the walls, dressed in a pair of Hawaiian-print swim trunks and wearing the water goggles and snorkel we'd picked up at the sporting goods store.

It was an off day and our team's former goalie, Drew, and his wife, Nina, were taking their kids, Wes and Hadley's two older kids and Joey, to an indoor water park for the day. Sawyer was picking Joey up and hanging with him at the water park since Joey wasn't a strong swimmer and he needed one-on-one supervision.

I would have gone, too, but Jolie was coming

over so we could talk. I was a wreck, though I was putting on a brave face for Joey.

She was either coming over here to try to work things out or to tell me it was over and she never wanted to see me again. I'd plead my case if it was the latter, but Jolie knew her own mind and I didn't think I stood much of a chance.

I missed her. I hadn't realized how much her texts throughout the day and our low-key movie nights with Joey meant to me until they were gone.

Jolie and I fit together perfectly. I just had to make her see it.

"Not yet, dude," I told Joey. "What do you want for breakfast?"

"Bacon and toast with strawberry jelly."

"You got it."

I took out the dishes to make breakfast and he slid onto a stool at the kitchen island with his iPad. We'd found a rhythm in our time together, and I was going to miss it. I hoped Emma and Joey would live with me, at least for a while, once we were all in Nashville.

I'd just finished cooking and cleaning up when Sawyer rang the doorbell.

"Is that bacon?" he asked, sniffing.

"Yeah, I made you some sandwiches."

He grinned. "Seriously?"

"Bacon, egg, and cheese. Two of 'em."

"Bro, you're the best wife ever."

Joey put a hand over his mouth to stifle his laugh, which did no good. I flipped Sawyer off as I looked through the bag I'd packed for Joey.

"Towel, change of clothes, cash, goggles, and snorkel. Am I forgetting anything?"

"Nope!" Joey tried to snatch the bag, but I held on to it.

"It's freezing out, Jojo. Go put on pants, a shirt, and your coat. And socks and shoes."

He groaned but then ran to his bedroom to do what I'd asked.

"Buzzkill," Sawyer quipped, grabbing a bottle of water from the fridge.

I was too wound up about Jolie to trade jabs with him.

"Hey, thanks for taking Joey," I said. "He's really excited if you didn't notice."

"No problem. I'm looking forward to it." He gave me a puzzled look. "You okay?"

"Yeah."

"Are you sick?"

I did feel like vomiting, but not because I was sick.

"Jolie's coming over," I said. "So we can have a talk."

"Oh shit. Are you ending things?"

I shook my head. "I'm not, but she might be."

"Because of Nashville?"

"Pretty much. It's a long story."

He put a hand on my shoulder. "Let me know if you want to talk about it."

"I won't. But thanks."

Joey ran back out to the living room, dressed now. He flew past us and went straight to the door.

"Can we go now?"

Sawyer laughed. "Yeah, let's go."

"Hey, be good," I said.

"I will," Joey said.

"Oh, I meant Sawyer."

Sawyer put his palms up. "I make no promises. Except that we'll have fun. You ready for some fun, my man?"

Joey jumped up and down. "Yeah!"

"Good luck," Sawyer said as he grabbed Joey's bag.

Once they were gone, I was alone with my dread. All I could do now was wait. Jolie was holding my future in her hands.

A FEW MINUTES LATER, I opened my door and found Jolie standing there, tears shining in her eyes.

Fuck. My stomach churned as I studied her expression.

"Hey," I said, reaching for her hand.

"Hey." She barely got the word out, her face crumpling as she took my hand.

I stepped aside and she came in. As soon as I closed the door behind her, I put my arms around her. She sank against me and I closed my eyes, inhaling the scent of her coconut shampoo. This was what I needed—to have her in my arms.

"I miss you," I said softly.

"I miss you, too."

She pulled away and looked up at me, wiping the corners of her eyes. "Can we sit down?"

I nodded, releasing her. My heart hammered as I watched her walk over to the couch. This couldn't be it. I wouldn't let it.

"Come with me," I said, my voice breaking.

I cleared my throat, hoping to get the words out without getting emotional.

"It's shitty of me to ask you," I continued. "You've been in school forever—your whole life, pretty much, and here I am asking you to follow me to my hometown, where I get to keep my job and you have no prospects."

She hadn't reached the couch yet when she turned to look at me, eyes widened slightly. I'd already started, so I figured I might as well go all in.

"I know all the reasons I shouldn't ask," I said. "You're about to finish your degree, you were engaged not that long ago, I'm going to be starting with a new team, we haven't been seeing each other that long."

She nodded but stayed silent.

"There's this one thing, though…" My voice faltered again and I looked away, trying to swallow the lump in my throat. "There's this one thing that makes all that other stuff not matter. I love you, Jolie. Maybe I'm a selfish bastard for saying it, but I love you and I want you to drop everything here and come to Nashville with me. Move in with me. Be with me."

She swiped at the corners of her eyes again and said, "You do?"

"Yeah. I want it a lot. And I know it's selfish. That's why I couldn't even say it before. Your family is here, you have all kinds of career opportunities here and everywhere else, but I'm asking you to leave it all behind. For me."

I held my breath as she wiped tears from her cheeks. Never in my life had I put myself out there like that for a woman. But if Jolie didn't come to

Nashville with me, I wanted to know I'd done everything in my power to get her to.

"So you'd want us to live together?" she asked.

"I know it's soon, but…yeah. I think we should. I'm not asking you to move so we can see each other once or twice a week. I want to see you every day I'm home, even if it's just for a few minutes on a busy day."

She blew out an exhale. "Wow. I had myself so convinced that you just wanted to move on."

I went to her, covering the distance between us and cupping her face in my hands. "I'm not great at talking about my feelings, but I'll work on it. I've always thought actions were the most important, but words matter, too."

"I could find a job in Nashville," she said. "If you want me to go with you, I can start looking."

"There's no *if*, Jolie. I want you with me. I love you."

She smiled then, her eyes dancing with happiness. "I love you, too. I know it's soon, and…all the other things you mentioned. I know my dad can be impossible, and I'll have to pass on both the New York and St. Louis job opportunities to find something in Nashville, but when I consider all the options, the one thing I can't stand the thought of giving up is you."

I slid my hand around to cup the back of her neck. "So that's a yes? You'll come?"

"Yes."

Fireworks exploded in my chest as I leaned in to kiss her. It started soft but quickly turned passionate; I was hungry for every inch of her. She pulled away all of a sudden, giving me a panicked look.

"Where's Joey?"

"He's at a water park with Sawyer."

Her shoulders sank with relief. "So it's just us?"

"Just us."

I grabbed the back of my shirt and pulled it up over my head, tossing it on the floor. Jolie's gaze skimmed over my naked torso, her eyes full of lust, as she pulled her shirt off too.

There was no way I'd ever tire of looking at her tits in the lacy little bras she wore. Her nipples stood out through the satin, begging for attention. I reached for the button on her jeans, my lips descending on her neck as I unfastened them.

"I missed that," she said in a breathy tone. "The way your scruff feels on my skin."

I slid her pants down, kissing her neck, her collarbone, and the spot behind her ear that drove her crazy. She fumbled with the button on my jeans, finally getting it undone and shoving them down, running her hands over my ass cheeks before giving them a squeeze.

"Meet me in your bed," she said, stepping back. "I want to be on top."

She darted in that direction and I followed, getting a view of her ass as she slid her panties off. I frantically pulled my boxers off, my cock aching for her. As I hustled after her into my bedroom, she unfastened her bra and let it fall to the floor, cupping her breasts and then sliding her hands down her body. I settled on my bed with my back against the headboard.

"Jesus, you're killing me," I said.

Finally, she got on the bed and straddled me, both of us groaning as she sank down onto my cock. I held her hips as she rode me hard and fast, quickly getting herself close to release.

It was all I could do to hold on as I looked up at her, her head tossed back and her nipples hardened into sharp points.

She moaned and I held tight to her hips as she ground herself against me, her sounds of satisfaction driving me over the edge with her.

When she slid off of me and curled up beside me, she put a hand on my cheek, gently turning my face until we were eye to eye.

"I love you, too," she said softly. "I didn't know

before what it meant to fall in love, but now I do. I feel powerless to stop the way I feel for you but safe at the same time."

I rested my hand on her lower back, our foreheads touching as we lay side by side. "That's exactly how I feel. It's kind of like a runaway train, but it's still on the tracks, so at least there's that."

She hummed her amusement and brushed her lips over mine gently. "I wish it could always feel like this."

"Maybe it can. I'm ready to find out with you."

"I can be slightly stubborn," she said. "What happens when we fight?"

"This. Makeup sex that makes us forget we were ever mad at each other."

"I can live with that," she said, her breath warm on my lips. "And it will probably be your fault every time we fight anyway."

"You think so, huh?"

"Happy wife, happy life," she said, cupping my cheek. "I mean, not anytime soon, obviously, but"

"I want to get there with you," I said, cutting her off. "I can picture you, me, and my family in our big kitchen in a decade, our own kids running around and raising hell."

"With you for a father, they'll be hellions for sure," she teased.

"*Our* hellions."

"With an equal passion for hockey and science."

I grunted, pretending to consider that. "How about nearly equal?"

"How about you kiss my ass?"

I grinned, giving her ass a mild slap. "There's the sassy redhead who stole my heart."

"I'm keeping it, by the way."

"It's all yours, babe. Now and always."

EPILOGUE

Jolie

ONE YEAR later

"YOU SURE ABOUT THIS?" Dad grumbled, scowling as my mother adjusted his tie.

"I've never been surer about anything," I replied, staring into the mirror as I thought about how my life had changed in the last year.

I looked pretty today. I didn't know if it was the dress, the professional hair and makeup, or simply the fact that I was marrying Boone, but I had a glow that was impossible to miss. I was so happy, so in love with the man I was about to marry, most of what I saw in the mirror reflected love. Hope. The future.

"You're beautiful," Mom whispered, coming to stand beside me.

"Thank you."

"The most beautiful bride ever," Grandma G said, her eyes filling with tears of happiness as she stood on my other side.

"I hope he knows how lucky he is," Dad grunted, watching us through the mirror.

I turned to him. "Dad, you *promised.*"

He held up his hands as if surrendering. "Yeah, yeah, I know. I just mean, I want you to be happy." He paused, blowing out a breath and staring up at the ceiling for a few seconds before focusing on me. "You're my only daughter, my only child. When we couldn't have any more, I vowed I would do everything in my power to make sure you had a good life. The best life. I guess, in retrospect, maybe I went a little overboard. Because I couldn't stand the thought of you being unhappy. Or someone hurting you. I thought I could prevent that just by being in control. I was wrong, but I hope you know how much I love you."

"I'm so happy, Daddy," I whispered, walking over to him. "He makes me happier than I ever imagined I could be. I promise."

He held out his arms and wrapped me in a huge hug. The same kind of hugs we'd share when I was a little girl, when he'd made me feel so safe.

We'd grown apart over the years, but somehow, now that I lived in Nashville, we'd gotten closer. We had lunch or breakfast when he was in town with the team. He made time for me when I went home to St. Louis to see Grandma G. We texted more regularly. For the first time in more than a decade, Dad and I had a relationship.

He still grumbled and complained now and then about Boone moving me "halfway across the country" to Nashville, even though it was only a six-hour drive, but he'd given his blessing when Boone had asked for my hand in marriage. I'd told him it was ridiculous and unnecessary—I was a grown woman who didn't need my father's permission—but Boone had insisted it was symbolically important.

To my surprise, it had gone a long way toward repairing their relationship. They talked once in a while now too, so we were making progress.

"Is everyone ready?" Sheridan stuck her head in the door. "It's time."

"We're going," Mom said, kissing me on the cheek before heading for the door.

Grandma G squeezed my arm as she passed me,

giving me a wink as she disappeared after my mother.

"The girls are ready," Sheridan stage-whispered. "Can I tell them to start?"

I nodded.

Boone and I had settled into our new life here in Nashville, but the Mavericks were still very much a part of our extended family. Sheridan, Hadley, and Sariah had drawn straws to see who would be my matron of honor because I hadn't been able to choose, Annalise was the flower girl, and though Andy was Boone's best man, he had Sawyer, Nash, Wes, and Lars in the wedding party. Joey was the ring bearer and Emma was also in the wedding party, so we'd somehow incorporated friends, family, and extended family into the wedding, which made us happy.

Despite my protests, this wound up being another massive event. It had been impossible to pare it down. Between the friends we'd made on the team here in Nashville, the Mavericks, our families, and my colleagues at my new job at Vanderbilt, the guest list had grown exponentially. Instead of just our families and a small group of close friends, over three hundred people were out in the church waiting for me to walk down the aisle, and I couldn't help but laugh as I thought about the last time I'd almost done this.

There would be no almost this time, though.

I loved Boone with everything I was.

"Ready, honey?" Dad asked, extending his arm.

"I am."

We walked into the anteroom, waiting for Annalise to walk ahead of me.

She was so excited and her eyes widened when she saw me.

"Jolie! You look prettier—"

"Shh." Dad put his finger to his lips. "It's your turn to go, sweetheart."

"I'm ready!" Her voice was no quieter, but her exuberance made me smile.

I watched as she tossed flowers in every direction, grinning at everyone she passed, whether she knew them or not.

Dad took a step forward and I realized this was it.

Holy shit.

I was getting married.

For a moment, I froze. A million memories of last year whiplashing through my mind, but then my gaze landed on Boone. In his white tuxedo, surrounded by his brother and teammates, he'd never looked as handsome as he did right now.

When his eyes found mine, even from across the massive room, there was no denying the spark.

The connection.

The love.

This man loved me as much as I loved him.

Everything else melted away as I took the first step toward forever.

———

THE EVENING FELT like a whirlwind of one event after the other. The ceremony, pictures, arriving at the reception, more pictures, dinner, speeches, another round of pictures, cutting the cake, and talking to people. There were so many people to talk to. Friends, family, Boone's teammates from all the teams he'd played for in his career, coworkers from both my current job as well as from the university in St. Louis. There were a lot of people here and everyone wanted our attention.

"You look amazing," Hadley said, hugging me. "I'm so happy for you both."

"Thank you."

"Did you tell her yet?" Sheridan asked, nudging her.

Hadley giggled.

"What's going on?" I asked.

"I'm pregnant," Hadley whispered.

"Really?" I asked in surprise.

"Aiden is thirteen months old, so he'll be almost two by the time this baby comes. We decided we didn't want there to be a huge gap between the four kids, so we started trying. But you can't tell anyone —I haven't even told Wes yet. It's going to be a surprise on our anniversary since it's next week."

"Congratulations." I hugged her again. Then I eyed Sheridan. "And you?"

She laughed. "Lars is still traumatized by the C-section. But he'll come around. I think we'll start trying later this year."

"You'll be back from your honeymoon before our wedding, right?" Lucy asked, coming over to join us. She and Konstantin were getting married in August.

"Of course." I squeezed her arm. "We wouldn't miss it."

"I'm thinking a baby next summer," Sheridan teased her.

Lucy rolled her eyes. "Have you been talking to Kon? He wants to get pregnant on the honeymoon."

I laughed. "Boone and I spend so much time with Joey, it's like we already have a kid."

Sheridan frowned. "How's Emma doing?"

"Honestly, she's doing well, determined not to fall off the wagon. We're really proud of her. She and

Joey just moved into their own place a couple of months ago, and she's gone out on a few dates recently, so things are looking up. But every day is a struggle. We try to help with Joey because we adore him, but also because it's important for her to have a little time to herself, you know? Being a single mom is hard."

"For sure," Hadley nodded. "I can't even imagine doing this on my own."

"Are you gossiping without me?" Sariah asked, joining us.

"Just updating Jolie on some of what she's missed since her last visit," Hadley said, winking.

"Have you and Nash set a date yet?" I asked Sariah.

She wrinkled her nose. "Between all the baby births, your wedding, and now Kon and Lucy's coming up, we haven't wanted to step on any toes. We're not in any hurry, though. We already live together, so there's no rush. When we start getting baby fever, we'll think about setting a date."

"I feel like whatever's going on here in this little circle is dangerous," Wes said, coming over to us and sliding an arm around his wife, his eyes twinkling with amusement.

"Whatever do you mean?" Hadley looked up at

him with an innocent look on her face and they both laughed.

We dispersed after that, and before I knew it, the DJ had called on Boone and me to have our first dance.

"Doing okay, beautiful?" Boone whispered in my ear as we started to move.

"I'm wonderful," I whispered back, gazing into his gorgeous blue eyes. "I just wish I had more than five seconds to enjoy my new husband."

"We're going to have two whole weeks alone in Fiji," he said. "We'll have so much time together, you're going to be sick of me."

"Never going to happen," I said softly. "Not in a million years."

"Have I told you how much I love you yet today?"

I twined my arms around his neck. "Once or twice. But I wouldn't mind hearing it again. And again."

"I love you so much. And I plan to spend the rest of my life showing you how much."

"Can you believe a year ago we didn't even know each other?"

"And then you freakin' carjacked me in the parking lot of a church." He pretended to look horrified.

"Best day of your life," I quipped, laughing.

His face softened as he gazed at me, the look of adoration in his eyes melting my heart. "Absolutely the best day of my life. Until today anyway. I love you, Mrs. Boone."

"Love you more, Mr. Boone."

Book 2 - Hard Limit

Book 3 - Hard Pass

Book 4 - Hard Luck

FIRE ON ICE SERIES

Book 1 - Bound

Book 2 - Captive

Book 3 - Edge

Book 4 - Drive

Book 5 - Release

ON THE LINE SERIES

Book 1 - Killian

Book 2 - Bennett

LOCKHART BROTHERS SERIES

Book 1 - Deep Down

Book 2 - In Deep

Book 3 - Drawn Deeper

Book 4 - Hidden Depth

FILTHY SERIES

Book 1 - Dirty Work

Book 2 - Dirty Secret

Book 3 - Dirty Defiance

Brenda Rothert lives in Central Illinois with her husband, children and two dogs. A former print journalist, she has written more than fifty romance novels. Her print and e-books have been translated into German, Italian and Portuguese, and her audiobooks have been translated into German.

She loves to hear from readers through her website or her Facebook Group, Rothert's Readers.

Zaan

Tore

Anton

Van

Decker

Alaska Blizzard:

Defending Dani

Holding Hailey

Winning Whitney

Losing Laurel

Saving Sara

Chasing Charli

A Very Blizzard Christmas

Tending Tara

Calling Cassie

Playing Peyton

Catching Lana (An Alaska Blizzard Companion Novel)

St. Louis Mavericks (with Brenda Rothert)

Hard Fall

Hard Limit

Hard Pass

Hard Luck

Lauderdale Knights:

Knight Before Christmas (A Garland Grove/Lauderdale Knights holiday novel)

Slap Shot

Big Shot

Long Shot

Hot Shot

Sure Shot

Rock Hard:

Play

Pause

Rewind

Fast Forward

The Royal Trilogy:

Nowhere Left to Fall

Nowhere Left to Run

Nowhere Left to Hide

Royal Protectors:

Sandor

Cocky Protector (book 1.5, part of the Cocky Heroes Club series)

Xander

Axel

Dax (*A Royal Protectors/Sidewinders crossover novel*)

Inferno:

Salvation's Inferno

Temptation's Inferno

Redemption's Inferno

Tropical Inferno (formerly "Tropical Ice")

Romancing Europe:

Adonis in Athens

Smitten in Santorini

Lucky in Lugano

View Kat's entire collection of books at
www.KatMizera.com

USA Today Bestselling author Kat Mizera was born in Miami Beach with a healthy dose of wanderlust. She's lived from coast to coast, and everywhere in between, but home is wherever her family is.

A devoted mom and wife to her wonderful and supportive husband (Kevin) and two amazing boys (Nick and Max), Kat loves to travel the globe with her adventurous, hockey loving family. Greece is at the top of that list. She hopes to one day retire there, spending her days writing books on the beach.

Kat is former freelance sports writer who now writes steamy hockey romance about her favorite fictional teams, the Las Vegas Sidewinders and the Alaska Blizzard. The library of novels she's penned also include sexy contemporary stories about base-ball stars, alpha sex club owners, special forces heroes, rock stars and royalty. Regardless of genre, her books about bad boys with hearts of gold will steal your breath, rock your world and melt your heart.

WHERE TO FOLLOW KAT:

WEBSITE
FACEBOOK
TWITTER
INSTAGRAM
BOOKBUB
KAT'S PRIVATE FACEBOOK GROUP